UNACCEPTABLE

AN UNACCEPTABLES MC ROMANCE

KRISTEN HOPE MAZZOLA

COPYRIGHT

File ID: 74093217 © nastia1983/ Dollar Photo Club

File ID: 51297995 © Monika Olszewska / Dollar Photo Club

Formatting by: Kristen Hope Mazzola

Editing by:

C. Marie editingbycmarie@gmail.com

❀ Created with Vellum

NOTE FROM THE AUTHOR

Thank you so much for picking up a copy of Unacceptable. I appreciate the time you spend allowing me to entertain you through my books. I genuinely hope you enjoy this story! If you do, please consider leaving a review! Reviews help authors!

Please note: This is meant for audiences that are 18+ for sexual situations, language, and adult content.

This story is not for the faint of heart! But if gore, violence, and extreme sexual situations are your cup of tea, this is the read for you.

"Kristen's sex scenes are HOT! I mean who doesn't like a built up bad boy biker with a dirty mouth...yeah ok no-one! Go grab this great little read ASAP! You won't regret it!"
- *Bookalicious Babes (Book Blog)*

"The story was unique for a stepbrother romance as there is a lot more to the story than them being step siblings. The back story is very interesting and different to the stepbrother stories I've read previously and this was a big plus for me with the story."
- *Author Groupies (Book Blog)*

"Kristen does a great job of writing characters that you want to see overcome the bad in their life and find their happy ending."
- *Amazon Reviewer*

"This was a fast read, yet had no absence of plot. Kristen knows how to write! Tastefully written, full of emotion, with a nice, sweet romance, not salacious at all!"
- *Maari Loves Her Indies (Book Blog)*

"The characters are perfection, the story line is not drama-filled just for the sake of a story, and there's just something special about it."
- *C from Prisoners of Print (Book Blog)*

DEDICATION

To everyone who has fought for love in their lives: Never let it go. It is precious and rare.

AN OUTLAW'S CODE:

Never say die and never give up.
Whether in a fight, debate, or curve too tight,
No matter how bad it gets, an outlaw never shows weakness
and never gives up.

THE UNACCEPTABLES MOTTO:

Fear none. Respect few.

UNACCEPTABLES MC LOGO

THE UNACCEPTABLES BAR AND POOL HALL LOGO

CHAPTER 1

S lam!

The sound of my mom throwing her hair dryer across their room and it crashing through the thin walls of our doublewide jolted me from my deep sleep.

"Why don't you just leave then, you fucking scumbag?" She was messed up again, slurring her words together as she picked another fight with my father after coming home in the early hours of the morning.

"Don't you freaking tempt me Helen, I swear to fucking God." My dad's raspy voice was low and gravely, probably trying to not wake me.

Too late.

This fight wasn't like every other night that she came home late from the bar; this one sounded worse.

"If you want to leave so badly, then just do me a damn

favor and get the hell out, you rat bastard." I heard their door open and the sound of my dad's boots stomping down the hallway with the light thudding of my mom trying to run after him in heels.

"Helen, get the hell off me. Enough is enough." He was right outside my door. I held my breath. I was ready to run away with him.

"You damn asshole you're not taking her with you!"

Slap!

Slap!

Slap!

I could hear her hitting him.

"You're not going to raise my daughter, you fucking, no good, whore. I'll leave her here over my dead body!" That was the first night I ever heard that word: whore. It was the perfect definition for my mother. It was exactly what she was.

I heard my mother's sobs getting softer as my dad slowly opened the door to my room. I held my breath, trying to pretend I was still asleep, silently begging him to pick me up in his strong arms and whisk me away from the trailer park and the terrible person that pretended to be a good mother.

"Yes. Hello." I heard her meek voice crack as she sniffled into the receiver of our old yellow corded phone in the kitchen. "My boyfriend is trying to kidnap my daughter. Please send someone fast."

"You damn—you goddamned cunt! She's my daughter too."

"Fuck you, Rave! If you wanted her to be your daughter so badly, you should have signed the damn birth certificate!"

The front door swung open and my father's boots trudged down the metal steps, the sound echoing in my ears as my heart got heavier with each stomp. I ran to the window and watched my hero, my savior, the only person that ever showed me love get in his truck and drive away.

Taillights. That's really what I remembered from that night. The glow of the taillights of my father's rusty, clunking white long-bed. The gravel spit out from under the tires as he ran away to his freedom. Who could blame him? Not me, that's for damn sure. I was about to follow in his footsteps. It had only taken me seventeen years to grow the metaphorical balls to realize that he was right. He had made the right move. All of the resentment and anger I had displaced onto him for abandoning me was finally falling on the right shoulders: hers, my fucking whore of a mother.

I sat outside the trailer I'd grown up in, in the same spot my dad had escaped from, watching the light switch off in my mom's room from the front seat of my beat up Camaro. She was probably over dramatically faking another orgasm while john-number-five-hundred-and-something believed every grunt and groan. I had to hand it to her: she was damn good at her job.

I took the worn pages of the letter I had read thousands of times and stuffed them back into the envelope. I read the city name in the return address again: *Vilas.* That's where I'd start my new life. That's where I'd start my search, not for him, but for myself. If it was good enough for my father, it'd be good enough for me.

It had been ten years since I'd gotten my only letter from him. It was my most cherished possession. I knew the whole thing by heart, but the last line stuck with me, like a broken record in my mind:

I have always loved you and I always will, never forget that, Princess.

Getting that handwritten note changed my life. It gave me hope, courage, and a fire under my butt to make something better of myself. In the back of my head I knew that it was only one short letter, that if he truly loved me like he had so dramatically claimed, he would have come back for me, fought for me, even stayed that night, but that was all in the past. It was time to start the future and for fuck's sake, I was about to take the bull by the horns and be something more than a trailer park critter that stripped to make ends meet.

The old engine cried to life after the third time I turned the key. I really needed to get it looked at, but I needed to get the hell out of the trailer park first. I had no plan, just a stack of uncashed paychecks from the Pink Kitty, where I had been working for years, and a wad of dollar bills that I had managed to hide from my mother, but it would have to be enough. I had hit the wall and was finally able to see it: I needed to move on.

I did have to give her some credit where it was due: my mom tried. She loved me in her own way, but she was never loving or motherly. She was either high or fucking to get her next fix for most of my childhood, but that was ok; I was over it. I'd realized long ago that you can't ask more of someone than they are capable of; she was nothing more than a hooker, and I had to accept it. My mom had no aspiration to make something more of herself and I would have to live with that. There is no saving someone that doesn't want to be saved, that's for damn sure.

I glanced back in my rearview mirror as the dusty road took me away from the only home I had ever known.

Hopefully this will be my last look at that hellhole.

I jammed out to Katy Perry and T-Swift while shifting and grinding gears as the road twisted and turned, my long black curls dancing in the wind coming in through the open windows. Liberation boiled in my veins while a sting of guilt bit at the back of my mind. I knew that she would figure out later rather than sooner that I had ditched her. It probably wouldn't be until she went to raid my room for my stash of money that I tried to hide from working all those damn late nights for nasty truckers and slime balls.

I drove and drove, stopping for gas a handful of times, having to fill up the clutch and power steering fluid on a few occasions, and ignoring my body's aching need for a bed. I desperately wanted to put as much road and as many states as humanly possible between me and the shithole I was crawling out of. Coffee and chocolate donut holes would have to do until I just couldn't take it any longer.

The day droned on and my eyelids got heavier and heavier as a slow Boyz II Men song poured from the speakers. That's when I finally saw it, the sign that I had been waiting for: "Vilas – 5 miles".

Heck yes!

I was as giddy as a schoolgirl as joy consumed me. I felt like I had finally made it. This wasn't just a dream built up in the mind of a naive child. It was real. I was finally free. I could fucking taste the sweet victory as I breathed in the dusty road that was leading the way to my salvation.

As I pulled off the highway and turned down a back country road, the exhaustion started to settle in deep. A yawn took over as I made my way into a dive-looking bar's parking lot. I needed to find a place to crash and figure out my next move. I grabbed the bright red lipstick from my bag; even though I felt and probably looked like shit, lipstick would make it a little better. Two things I never left the house without: a good bra and lipstick.

A handwritten "Help Wanted" sign caught my eye as I pulled on the worn metal handle. The smell of cigarette smoke wafted out as I swung the heavy wooden door open. It felt like an old movie where the music cuts out when the main character mistakenly walks into a bar that outsiders aren't welcome in. There were a few empty bar tables scattered around and a handful of pool tables in the back.

I took a seat at one of the creaking swivel barstools at least five seats away from the next patron. Every eye was glued on me as I threw my purse down on the bar with a thud and waved to the older bartender. It made me a little bit more uneasy when I realized I was the only person with a vagina in the whole joint. A few of the guys at the pool table behind me nearly broke their necks as I walked in with my tight skinny jeans, pushup bra, and flowy yoga top.

The bartender meandered over my way while I got a good look into his kind honey eyes; his shaved bald, shiny head; and the pure white, long handlebar mustache that rested over his curling lips. His rosy cheeks made him look far more jolly than he probably was. What really caught my eye was the cut that he was wearing. I'd definitely wandered into the wrong bar where outsiders were not welcome in the slightest.

I took a deep breath and reminded myself that I was a tall skinny chick and that my gun was only a foot away in my handbag. After working as a stripper for the better part of five years, I'd learned quickly that I needed to know how to protect myself and to not let fear ever cross my face.

In a slow drawl, his voice cracked the silence, "Can I get you somethin', sweetheart?"

I swallowed hard before answering, "A bottle of Bud Light, please." I felt like a mouse would have spoken louder than I just had, but he nodded and reached into the ice trough in front of him to grab my beer.

"Do I know you from somewhere?" His pale honey eyes narrowed; he was studying my face pretty intently. I glanced over to my bag where the only letter that I had from my father was concealed next to my three-eighty bodyguard. He very well could be in this bar or know this bartender. The town was small enough.

I shook my head. "I've never been here before."

"I think I would remember meeting you." He winked with a throaty chuckle before looking over to help a man in a matching cut that just had sat down next to me.

The newcomer ordered his whiskey on the rocks and leisurely turned in my direction. I glanced at the back of the bartender just long enough to read the club's name scrolled across the back: The Unacceptables. Glancing over, my cheeks flared red as I took in the features of the young biker to my right. Everything faded into a blurry background when the extremely tall, broad-chested stud smiled at me. His lips were the perfect shade of light red, pierced with two small hoops in the left corner, and even his eyes smiled as his gaze met mine.

"Hello there." He slid his stool closer to mine.

I shook my head quickly, trying to get my wits about me while his deep blues were threatening to drown me. "Hi." I sipped from my beer slowly, fighting to hide how nervous I had become all of a sudden.

"Not from around here are you?" The bartender slid his drink in front of him.

"Nope. Just passing through."

I read the words "vice president" on the front of his cut before I let my mind start to focus completely on how breathtakingly handsome this man truly was.

Slow. Deep. Breaths.

Slow.

Deep.

Don't let him catch you practically drooling.

Damn, he's gorgeous.

"That's a shame." His lip curled under his piercings as his tongue rolled over the silver hoops gently. "I'm Abel." He held out his hand for me to take.

"Nice to meet you, I'm Crickett."

"Wait." He tried desperately not to laugh as his cheeks got red and his lips pulled up at the corners. "Your name is Crickett? Like chirp chirp?"

"Yep, it sure is." I rolled my eyes before taking a long swig from the bottle. "I'm named after a damn insect."

"Who would ever think to name their kid that?" He was full blown laughing now as the hilarity of my unfortunate name really sunk in deep.

"A deadbeat and a hooker."

The bartender practically jogged down the bar after my name hit the air and gave Abel a stern look. "Table. Now!"

"Everything all right, Bucky?"

The gruff old man narrowed his eyes. "The meeting was supposed to start fifteen minutes ago, son. I'll be up in a second. Rich is looking for ya."

Another bartender without a cut on slid behind the bar and all of the bikers filed through a door at the back of the bar. Abel was gone in a flash, without the slightest goodbye.

The young guy—who couldn't be much older than eighteen judging by his patchy beard mixed with peach fuzz—walked over to me. "Miss? Care for another?" He pointed at my almost empty bottle and I nodded.

After taking a sip of the fresh icy cold amber goodness, I looked up at the guy playing on his phone. "Do you know a good motel close by?"

He smiled, glancing up from the screen. "Oh yeah, we have one just a block north of here, right off the main road. Can't miss it."

"Great, thanks. What's your name?" I felt chatty, even bored, and I was great at flirty small talk. I figured, why not chat up this cutie and hopefully get some details about Abel?

"Me? I'm Holt."

"Oh crap, I almost forgot." I dug the koozie out of my purse and placed it on my beer.

Holt's eyebrow raised.

"What? You don't want cold hands or warm beer."

"Yeah. I guess you're right."

"Are you from around here, Holt?" I twirled a long curl between my fingers and stared into his dark brown eyes.

"Born and raised." His drawl was thick as he wiped the bar top with a wet towel. "What about you?"

"I'm from a few states over. Making a break for it." I chugged half my beer.

"Running ain't always a bad thing. Vilas is a good town. Hopefully you'll like it here."

"How much do I owe you for these?"

I bit my lip slowly and watched Holt's cheeks flare as he rubbed the back of his neck and stuttered a bit. "It was taken care of." He held up his hand to stop me from taking my wallet out of my purse.

I raised my eyebrow at him. "Really?"

He nodded. "Abel told me to put it on his tab. So you're good to go."

Wow. Sweet, mysterious, and hot. I might have to give this town and Abel a trial run.

"Thanks, Holt. Maybe I'll see you around."

He nodded. "Hope you get some rest."

"I look that bad, huh?"

Holt smiled sweetly as he shook his head. "Nah, you just look like you've been traveling for a while and need a hot shower and a bed."

"Well then I look the way I feel. That Abel guy, he's all right?" I should have been more subtle, but I was worn out and beating around the bush seemed more draining than what it was worth.

"Yeah, he's one of the best guys I know. Tough skin but a fucking heart of gold."

"Good to know." I chugged the rest of my beer and threw a couple dollars on the bar. Holt's sweet smile spread wider as the guys came back out from the backroom, or abyss, or wherever they'd all run off to in such a hurry. To my dismay, Abel was not in the group that filed back into their bar seats. I waved goodbye to Holt and made my way to finally get the shuteye that I desperately needed.

CHAPTER 2

Rounding the corner, I saw the neon vacancy light shining bright above the motel's front office door. The dimly lit gravel parking lot crunched under the tires of my crying car. It was time to put more power steering fluid in for sure. I grabbed the plastic bottle of fluid from the floorboard of the passenger side and fixed the problem. At least there were a few things I could do under the hood of my car to make it run at a somewhat decent level. Growing up where most of the guys around built mud trucks had its perks from time to time.

Looking around as I made my way into the office, I noticed a few cars scattered around the lot, all with out of state plates. It was nice to know that other out-of-towners stopped there. It shouldn't have made a difference, but it comforted me to know that other travelers felt safe enough to crash there too.

The bell chimed above my head as I walked into the small office that smelled like mothballs and stale pizza. A sweet girl peeked up from a school book the was laid out on the counter. "Hey miss. Lookin' for a room?"

I nodded. "Sure am."

"Smoking or nonsmoking?"

Even though I was a smoker, the thought of stale cigarette smoke embedded in the pillows made me want to hurl on the spot.

"Nonsmoking."

"All right. I just need a credit card to hold the room. How many nights will you be our guest?"

For not being more than thirteen, she was very articulate and polite. I was pretty impressed by her.

"I'm not sure, actually." I dug my hands into my pockets; it felt unnerving as hell to not have any plan whatsoever.

"Longer than a week?"

I shrugged. "Possibly."

"We have weekly specials, you'll save fifty bucks that way."

"Sounds like a plan to me."

"Perfect." She punched a few keys on the dinosaur of a computer that was in front of me. "If anything changes, just come on in and let us know." Her kind eyes and sweet smile settled down my growing nerves as she handed me a key with a giant red plastic ornament-looking keychain on it.

"You're on the first floor, three doors over on the left."

I handed her my credit card and license. "All right, Miss Hayes. You're all set."

"Thanks." With a quick wave, I was off to finally lie down in a bed for a much needed night's sleep, even though it was still the afternoon.

———

THE LIGHT SHINING through the window stung my tired eyes as I groggily started to wake up. I had no idea what time I had actually crashed the day before. I'd barely even had time to turn the lights off before I hit the pillow and passed out, let alone undress, take off my makeup, or look at the clock.

Rolling over, bright red numbers blared eleven fifteen at me as my stomach started to rumble. After peeling myself from the pillow-topped mattress that felt like a lumpy heaven, I dug through the duffle bag that contained my life until I found my favorite pair of jeans and a yoga top.

I glanced at the bright red smear on the pillow from my favorite lipstick and the black dots from my mascara.

Thankfully I was not the one that was going to have to wrestle with those stains.

Within minutes the faucet was pumping steaming water into the tub. A nice long soak felt like a dream for my tired body. The trip hadn't been emotional until it all crashed onto me as I sunk to the bottom of that porcelain bath. I was free. I was finally freaking free, and I felt bad about it.

The image of my mom figuring out that I was gone broke into my mind and ripped my heart apart. But who was I kidding? If she hadn't started blowing up my phone yet, she had no idea. She was probably still in a haze of meth and booze from another week-long binge.

Right before I left, I could tell that's where she was heading anyway. It was the perfect time to escape: I would be so far gone by the time she was halfway conscious that it wouldn't matter.

"Critter!" Her hollow cry came from the back bedroom.

I rolled my eyes at her dumbass nickname for me. Wasn't my real name bad enough?

"Yeah Ma?"

"Get me a fucking coke from the fridge."

I grabbed the last can of soda from the barren wasteland she called a refrigerator.

I hurriedly popped the top and walked it back to her where she was laying in bed, sick as a dog from yet another withdrawal.

"Here. I gotta get to work."

Her shaking hand wrapped around the can as her sunken, dark eyes begged me for mercy. She didn't have to ask; I knew what I needed to do.

"Yeah. I think Vinnie is working tonight. I'll see what I can get."

"That's my girl. Thank you, Crit."

"I'll be back late though. Try to sleep and don't let anyone come over with you sick like this. I don't want this place to get robbed again."

I snapped out of my daze of strolling down terrible memory lane when the sound of splattering water echoed in the tiny bathroom. Looking over the side of the tub, I realized about half an inch of water was starting to coat the off white tiles.

Shit.

I lunged for the faucet, turned off the water, and sunk back in to relax and let my fingers and toes get pruney. I couldn't remember the last time I'd had time to relax like that. The quiet and the peacefulness were almost disturbing. It was a far cry from the cursing, fighting neighbors and my mom hollering at me or moaning in some john's ear all the time.

Good riddance to all that bull crap.

Giving in to my roaring stomach, I drained the water and got dressed. I laid towels on the floor of my soaking wet bathroom to lap up the water that had spilled over.

I made my way to the closest Waffle House my phone's GPS could find. Luckily it was just up the road and I had a hankering for greasy cooking and a pot of coffee. I quickly scarfed down some scattered, smothered, covered, and chunked hashbrowns with two eggs over easy on the side and tried to think about what my next move was going to be.

Not having a plan was both liberating and frustrating. I knew that the money I had was going to go faster than I could admit to myself. I checked the classified section for jobs while I sipped on hours-old coffee. I wasn't really built to be a stable hand, and I didn't think there was a strip joint in Vilas.

As I was getting up to pay my check, Holt and the older bartender walked through the front door. Holt ambled over to me with a sweet smile on his face.

"Nice to see you haven't left our little town yet. Thinkin' about sticking around?" He spit into a Dixie cup and I could smell the wintergreen chew that was wadded up in his lower lip.

I held up the paper and shrugged. "A girl's gotta eat and there ain't any jobs here for me it seems."

"Hey Bucky, aren't we still looking for a daytime bartender?"

He nodded. "Yeah, the one Abel hired last week quit on me Monday night."

"Well there ya have it. I'll talk to Abel about it. Come by in a few hours and we'll get ya all set up."

Just like that I had a freaking job in a town I wasn't even sure I was going to stay in. At least I knew I was going to be able to keep a roof over my head and hopefully finance another move, if nothing else.

CHAPTER 3

After going back to the motel, making sure my makeup was perfect, and changing my outfit at least ten times, I went to the bar to see if Holt had been able to talk Abel into hiring me.

"Hey, Crickett," Holt called to me from behind the bar. "Abel should be here any minute. Just got off the phone with him."

"Yeah? How'd it go?"

Holt was counting the register's drawer. He glanced up from a wad of twenties. "I think he is interested."

"Sounds good." I took a seat at the bar, throwing my purse on the counter with a big thump.

Holt stared at my bag for a second. "Do ya have rocks in there or something?"

I laughed a little. "Never seen a girl with a concealed carry before?"

"Yeah, but none that looked like you."

I felt my cheeks burn as the front door swung open. Abel's large frame took up most of the doorway. My heart pounded in my ears, my palms started sweating, and suddenly it was stifling hot in the dank bar.

"So Holt here says you're looking for a job?" Abel took the seat next to me; the musky smell of his cologne and his deep blue stare were all too distracting.

I fumbled for words. "Yeah, figured I'd give this little town a try for a bit. Who knows? Maybe I'll end up liking it here."

"When can you start?"

"Now."

He smirked. "Have you ever worked in a bar before?"

I laughed a little. I kind of had, but I'd been dancing, not pouring the drinks. "Something like that."

I winked and watched his mind try to make sense of it. "I guess that's good enough for me. Holt can start training you now, if that works for you."

I hopped off the stool and didn't think twice about going behind the bar to let Holt start showing me around.

"Damn it, isn't one of you going to ask if your boss wants a freaking beer?" Abel half-smirked at me as Holt tossed a bottle over to him from the ice trough in front of us. Opening the bottle, Abel got up and started to make his way to the back room. "That's more like it. And Crickett," he pointed at me with the top of the bottle, "this area is off limits to anyone that isn't wearing a damn cut like mine. Got it?"

I nodded.

His lip curled under the silver rings as he pulled the door open. "Good."

———

AFTER A FEW DAYS of working at the bar, I started to get to know most of the guys: which ones tipped well, which ones were drunk flirts, which ones treated chicks like dirt. It was all pretty much like stripping, other than the fact that the guys had to use their imaginations to know what my curves looked like rather than just trying to bribe me to get stark naked during a lap dance. All in all it was a welcome change of pace.

Only a few women passed through with their guys from time to time. Most of them just ignored me or were so snarky that I didn't give them the time of day. The only lady I remotely had an interest in talking to was Ronda, the part-time night bartender who only came in on nights that she felt like it, or when Abel called her in when Holt or Rich were too slammed to think straight.

She was tall and crack-head skinny with leathery

skin, nice as could be with a mouth like a sailor. Other than that, I had no female contact, which I actually preferred. Women bred drama and problems and I wanted to stay as far as humanly possible from both of those things.

While cleaning a bunch of dirty pint glasses off the bar I heard Abel talking to one of the older club members. "Rave will be gone handling everything for a few more days. Hopefully it all works out."

"Sure it will. Rave has a way with those guys over in Arkansas."

Hearing the name Rave and my home state in the same sentence sent shivers down my arms. I had no idea if it was just a coincidence; it probably was. *Right?* I could not picture my father being part of a motorcycle gang, but who the fuck was I to make any judgements either way? I barely remembered him, let alone knew him. He could have been sitting in that very bar and I would have had no idea.

"Crickett?" Abel waved his hand in front of my face. "Crickett, you all right sugar?"

I shook out of my daze of trying to picture my old man's face again. It scared the shit out of me how hard it was to remember his physical features anymore.

"Yeah." I smiled and stretched out my back. "Need another whiskey?" I pointed to the empty glass in front of him.

He shook his head. "We have to get out of here. Won't be too long."

He and the older guy got up with a few of the other men sitting at the bar. They all pulled cash out of their wallets, paid, and went on their way.

"You going to be okay here for a few hours? I need to go take care of some other shit for a bit."

Holt started wiping up the counter and throwing the empty beer bottles into the trash.

"Yeah. Sure. I'll be fine."

"I'll be back later to finish out the night shift so you don't have to work another double."

I shrugged. "Can't complain about the money. Do what you have to do."

My shift was pretty uneventful. A few of the regulars popped in and out, but there was nothing to write home about until a group of guys walked in. They looked to be a few years older than me and were completely out of place with their grungy, messy-but-put-together-messy look. Their hair and outfits were like controlled chaos.

The five-some took seats right in front of me at the empty bar.

"What are y'all havin'?"

"Do you guys have PBR?"

They were all tattooed and incredibly good looking, with an accent that I could not place.

I nodded. "Five PBRs coming up, boys."

After setting their beers down, curiosity got the better of me. "So what brings y'all to this neck of the woods?"

The guy on the end, who had a mohawk and tattoos on his skull, looked up from peeling the label off his bottle. "We're in a band. Playing in a show tomorrow night right up the road."

"Are y'all like famous or somethin'?"

The guy next to him, who had a sweet, seductive face, smirked. "I guess you could say that."

"So what band are y'all with?"

Tatted-Skull guy chimed in again. "We're The Hysterics. I'm Maverick, this is Colt, Dane, and Rodney. And that guy on the end is Quinn, our head roadie. We're playing a concert at App State."

The guys started chatting among themselves as the front door swung open. Abel strode in with Holt and a few other members following closely behind. Holt came back behind the bar and the rest went to the pool tables.

"You good?" Holt leaned over my way, grabbing beers to bring to Abel's group.

"Yeah. Go hang out for a bit if you want. It's been dead all day. I'll stick around a little longer."

He glanced over at the five guys. "You sure?"

Holt had an edge about him that I hadn't seen before. He was usually quiet but sweet, not edgy and protective.

I nodded. "Yes. Now get out of here before you lower my tip." I batted my eyelashes dramatically and shoved

Holt's shoulder. Out of the corner of my eye I thought I saw Abel's jaw churning while his eyes bored holes in Holt, but by the time my gaze snapped to meet his, Abel was winking at me, flashing his killer smile.

Weak knees.

Heart pounding.

Lady parts begging for me to tackle him onto that pool table.

After about an hour of chatting up the band members and roadie and catching Abel looking at me more and more, the flirty side of me decided to take over. Part of me wanted to see how jealous I could make Abel and the other part was just plain bored.

"Do any of you boys have a smoke I can bum?"

Quinn, the least good looking one out of them all, slid off his barstool and dug a pack of cowboy killers out of his front pocket. "Mind if I join you?"

I shook my head, walking around the bar toward the door. "The company is welcomed." I turned to call over to Holt, "Going for a quick smoke. Watch the bar?"

Holt nodded and Quinn and I were out the door with lit cigarettes within seconds.

"So how does a chick like you get to be working in a dive bar like this? Shouldn't you be a model or something?"

Talk about laying it on thick straight out of the gate.

I forced a flirty giggle, twirling my hair as I let out a

puff of white smoke, making sure I was standing right in the window in direct view of Abel, who was deliberately not looking our way. "I'm new in these parts. Gotta pay the bills somehow."

He ashed and the wind whisked it right onto the bottom of my shirt. "Oh shit sorry." He started to brush the grey off for me, taking a step closer—way closer than I would have wanted him to, but I was kind of flirting so who could blame him for trying to make a move?

I giggled again. "It's nothing really."

"I'm such a goof."

He took a step closer. I could smell the beer on his breath.

Gross.

"You should come to the show tomorrow night. You could hang out backstage with me." He leaned in a little closer. Kneeing him in the crotch crossed my mind for if he tried to touch me again.

I took a step back, crashing against the brick wall next to the window. His hand landed on my hip and I was ready to take a swing. Right then, Abel busted through the door like a bat out of hell, fire blazing in his eyes.

He stomped over and without a word, his fist landed square on Quinn's jaw.

I gasped. "Abel, what the hell?" I shoved him. "Wrong move."

His eyes narrowed as he stared at me. "This drunk asshole is not going to hit on you in my bar."

Quinn bowed up a little and Abel growled. "Do something about it, punk. I fucking dare you."

I watched as Abel's jaw flexed and Quinn's fists tightened while he stood there silent like a little pansy.

I put my hand on Quinn's chest. "Let's get some ice on that before it swells. Abel here needs to learn some goddamn manners."

I had to at least play pissed, even though I was silently thanking Abel for keeping me from having to be the one to defend myself. I knew that I had brought it on myself, but can't a girl have a smoke with a guy without him trying to get into her pants?

Before I could even take a step, Abel's hand was on my arm. "You," he pointed at Quinn, "get your damn friends and get the hell out of here." He turned to me. "I need a moment alone with my *employee*." He snarled as his grip got a little tighter than necessary.

I was ready to start yelling. Who the hell did he think he was, pulling a damn stunt like that? He didn't own me.

Quinn practically ran into the bar, right as I was starting to raise my voice to my sex-on-a-stick boss that had never been more attractive to me than in that moment.

"Abel! What in God's name do you think you're doing?"

He spun me around and pressed me up against the wall, pinning me between his rock solid chest and the bricks.

His voice was low as his hot breath danced on my neck. "I think that guy was no good and I was protecting what's mine."

"You don't own me, Abel."

"We'll see about that, sugar. I get what I want."

If he only knew that he could have had me before pulling a stunt like this. Other than the quick glances and the short comments, he'd never shown any interest in getting in my pants.

Well this escalated quickly.

Even though I was pissed, my heart raced and desire for him to take me right there coursed through my veins.

"What are you saying, Abel? That you want me? Newsflash, you're supposed to let people know when you want them, not stare at them from across the bar and never talk to them."

His lips got within an inch of mine. I braced myself for a kiss that never came. If I was a dude, I would have had blue balls. I definitely had the lady equivalent as my throbbing clit begged for him to press me harder against that wall.

"Everyone can tell, Crickett. It's not just about keeping our mouths shut. They can see it all over my face and yours. You're mine. And that is that."

"Keeping our mouths shut about what? Abel are you shitfaced or something?"

The door next to us swung open as the five guys nearly ran out of the bar, pissed and yelling at the roadie for being a fucking idiot and getting them kicked out of another bar.

Maverick waved over at us. "Sorry for the trouble. He's an ass." They all climbed into a rental car before Abel could start yelling. I guess musicians aren't really tough-guy-bar-brawl types, wouldn't want to break a hand right before a show. That would really suck some big ole monkey balls for sure.

Holt followed them out with a concerned look on his face. "Abel. They need you inside. Now."

Lady blue balls for sure.

"We'll finish this later." Abel jogged into the bar after Holt and vanished into the abyss in the back.

With the bar empty and my nerves pretty rattled, I called it a night. I grabbed my bag and got my tips out of the jar, and decided to head to my cozy motel room. My vibrator was undeniably going to be making an appearance that night.

CHAPTER 4

I turned the key in my jalopy of a Camaro and…nothing.

Clunk.

Click.

Clunk.

Click.

Damn it all to fucking hell.

I popped the hood and leaned into the engine, praying that I would see a loose valve or a miracle would happen. I knew deep down that there wasn't jack shit I could do to fix it. I was probably looking at a shot starter or something frustratingly expensive to fix.

"Hey do you need some help?" Looking over my shoulder, I saw Abel's tall frame ambling over to me from his motorcycle.

I rolled my eyes and leaned back over my engine. "What's it to you?"

"Hey, what's with the attitude?"

Abel's boots crunched on the gravel as he got closer and closer; my stomach knotted and churned.

What the hell is happening to me?

I spun on my heels and glared at him with a furrowed brow. "Your awesome douchebag stunt last night, ring a bell?"

He let out a deep throaty chuckle. "I was drunk and I saw a pretty girl getting hit on by a hipster. Can you blame me for being a little jealous?"

"You were totally out of line."

"So do you want help with this or not?"

I sighed. I was at a loss. "Yeah. I think so." I groaned, leaning on my front bumper.

"For what it's worth, I'm sorry for last night." His hand landed on my shoulder for a fleeting moment and my heart fluttered.

Deep breaths.

Deep.

Slow.

How does he continue to do this to me?

"Thank you."

"So what's going on here?"

I nodded at my busted, annoying-as-shit, piece-of-dog-crap engine. "She's ready to kick the bucket."

He rubbed the back of his neck as he leaned over the engine. "Mind if I take a look?"

Before I could even respond, he was under my hood, poking and looking around.

"It's been giving me some problems starting and this morning it's only clicking."

"Hmmm." He wiped his face with his flannel sleeve as he stood up straight. "Try to start her up?"

His dark blues choked me as they bore into mine for a second. "S-sure."

Even though I wanted to still be pissed about how he'd acted the night before, I couldn't help but feel flattered. Sure I had liked guys in the past, found some attractive, but I was always the take 'em and leave 'em type of girl, never sticking around long enough to get hurt or form real feelings. This felt different. It felt real. There was a spark that had been lit the day I walked into the Unacceptables' bar and it was smoldering into a wildfire that I felt the control of slipping out of my grasp.

I dove into the driver's seat and turned the key.

Click.

That's all she wrote.

"Again!" He shouted from around the popped hood.

Click.

"All right."

Abel came around to the open door and leaned on it. "I'm pretty sure you're gonna need a new starter. We can try to push start it since it's a stick, but I really don't think that's the answer to your problems."

"Fuck," I whispered to myself. "That's going cost a lot more than I can afford right now."

"It doesn't have to." His lips turned up at the corners before he continued, "I can take care of it for you."

I jumped up from my moping in the driver's seat. "Yeah? Really?"

He nodded, his smile growing, showing off his perfectly chiseled facial features.

Damn, he's hotter than a swamp in Mississippi in August.

"You don't think that bar is the only thing I take care of do you?"

I shrugged. "You've never mentioned anything before."

"Well, sugar, I run a garage a few miles from here. How about you let me take you to breakfast while one of my guys comes and tows this to the garage?"

My original reaction was to run, thinking this guy was too good to be true. He surely had to be a freaking serial killer or something, but damn those eyes, his smile, the muscles that his grey flannel shirt clung to so perfectly under his cut.

Even though he had been my boss for almost a week, I barely knew him. His time at the bar was fleeting, and in that moment I found myself doing something I had never done before: taking help from a stranger—a beautiful stranger, and my boss, but a fucking stranger never-theless.

"Ok."

"Let me make a call. Leave the keys in it. My guys will be here quick to get it for you."

"That's really nice of you, Abel."

"Don't mention it, Crickett." He laughed after he said my name, which was more common than I would have liked to admit.

"Don't be mean," I called over while he paced as he spoke to someone from his garage, lighting a cigarette.

"No. I am telling you what you're going to do." Smoke escaped through his flared nostrils as he growled into the phone. "Get your ass down here with Lou and pick up her car now. Not after you eat your damn breakfast or take your morning shit. Right the fuck now. Do you forget who you work for?"

Abel's voice was so gruff and stern while he was talking to whoever it was on the phone; I was kind of taken aback.

Once the call was over, I walked over to Abel. "You know if this is any trouble, I can figure something out."

"Really, could you?" His voice was still stern as he shoved his cell into his pocket, throwing the half gone cigarette into the gravel and mashing it with his boot. He cleared his throat before he continued, cooling his tone quite a bit. "This is no trouble at all, Holt was just being a little prick. Sometimes you have to put the young guys in their place."

"Holt? He works at your garage too?"

"Yeah, he works with you and is apprenticing at my garage. Good kid, just needs direction."

"Oh shit. My shift." It had slipped my mind; the whole reason I'd been trying to start my car was to grab some groceries before I had to be at the bar at noon.

Abel put his hand on my shoulder. "I'll make a call."

He walked a few steps away from me. "Holt. Change of plans. Tell Lou to get a guy with him over to Crickett's car. You're taking her day shift today."

Abel walked back over and flashed his killer triumphant smile. "Done. Now let's go eat. I'm starving."

I stared at his bike pretty nervously; I had never ridden on one before. Apparently it was written on my face. "Ever been on one of these before?"

I shook my head.

"This will be fun then." He grabbed a second helmet from the back compartment. "Here." He handed one over to me. "I'm going to get on first and then help you on, ok?"

I nodded. Holy hell, I was nervous. First week of truly being on my own and my car was broken down and I was about to spend the morning with a member of a motor-cycle gang who I fucking worked for. When I'd left home, this was not what I had pictured at all.

What the hell is going on?

"Put your arms around me. Hang on tight."

"Well, you don't have to tell me twice." I nervously laughed, flinging my arms around his middle as fast as I could.

"Don't be nervous."

From my shoulders all the way to my toes, I was tense. *How on God's green Earth does he expect me to not be nervous?*

Abel pulled my hands more around him until my fingers were locking, then rested his on mine for a second. "Trust me."

He pulled out of the parking lot where I left my car, keys in the ignition, and we were on our way down the road heading to an unknown destination. Even though I was pretty nervous, completely out of my comfort zone, that shit was pretty exciting. I knew it was high time for me to be this free and the wind whipping through my hair while my arms were wrapped around Abel's Adonis-like frame made me feel that much more liberated.

We pulled into a parking lot of a tin-can-looking building with a bright flashing neon sign: 24-Hour Diner.

Abel helped me off the bike. "They have the best milk-shakes in town."

My knees were shaky and I almost fell over, stumbling right in into Abel's side and practically tripping both of us.

"Hey, I got ya." He wrapped his arm around me. "That happens a lot when people ride a bike for the first time. To the milkshakes!" he exclaimed as we made our way up the steps to the front door.

"Thanks." I couldn't help the wide ass grin that was taking over my entire face. The whole situation was making me happier than it should have. I should have been pissed about my car and the night before, but actually I was excited to spend time with my beautiful stranger.

We sat in a booth and I started to look over the menu, but Abel quickly took it from me.

"Hey!" I grabbed for it but he snatched it out of my reach.

"Let me order for you. Trust me."

"There you go with that 'trust me' shit again. Have you forgotten that I don't even know you? Or that you cock blocked me last night?"

"Cock blocked? Really? You would have slept with that douche-nuzzle?" He narrowed his eyes, crossing his arms over his chest.

I shrugged. "Probably not, but it would have been nice to make my own decision about that instead of being thrown into a wall by my boss who I have barely had a full conversation with, then being informed that he has it in his head that he has some sort of claim over me."

"Well, if you don't feel the connection yet, I'll give you

some time. Let's start with the basics and get to *know* each other."

The waitress brought over two coffees and asked us if we knew what we were having. Abel looked at me and I waved my hand. "I'll have whatever he suggests."

"Two chocolate mint milkshakes and southwestern omelets, June. Thanks."

"You got it, Abel."

With a warm smile, June headed off to the kitchen.

"Come here a lot?"

Shaking sugar from the big clear cylinder into his coffee, he nodded. "My mom used to work here when I was a kid, so I've spent a lot of time right here in this booth."

I grabbed the sugar from him and cleared my throat. "So, you were about to tell me about yourself."

"Hmm." He nodded with coffee in his mouth. He swallowed quickly then dove in. "I'm from here. I'm an only child. My favorite color is green. I love mint, and that's why they have a chocolate mint shake here. Your turn."

I took a deep breath, wondering how deep into my situation I should get. "Well, let's see. My favorite color is blue, all kinds of blue. I don't know what my natural hair color is because I have been dying it since I was twelve. I love chocolate and mint together so I am pretty stoked to be trying this amazing milkshake."

June came back with two huge glasses of chocolaty goodness. "The omelets will be up soon."

"Thank you." I smiled while eyeing the large shake in front of me. It was a meal in and of itself; I should have refused the omelet for sure.

Abel was just sitting there, staring. "Are you going to drink yours?" I laughed a little while putting a straw into my milkshake.

"I'm waiting to see what you think."

His deep ocean eyes were breathtaking. I loved sitting there; it made it completely acceptable to stare at them.

"Well, here goes nothing."

I took a sip and it was like an orgasm in my mouth. I even moaned. Out. Loud.

My cheeks burned as I looked up to Abel.

"I told you."

I smiled, wiping my mouth. "That might be better than sex."

"Darlin', if you think this is better than sex, you've been fucking the wrong guys."

"I probably have been and there have been so few, I'm probably not a very good judge." I laughed. "I can't believe I just told you that."

He shrugged. "We're not strangers anymore."

"No, I guess we're not."

"So where are you from, Crickett?"

I swallowed hard again. Talking about my past was

awful but I knew I needed to get over it. I was in a small town where people asked questions and genuinely wanted to know the answers. Abel's gorgeous eyes were fixated on mine as his lips curled around the end of his shake's straw. We were having a light conversation, he just wanted to get to know me; I hated how scared I was to even mention the shithole that I was only days from climbing out of.

Deep breaths.

Smile.

Pretend like you're not scared shitless to let words fall into the air.

"Arkansas."

His eyes got a little wide as the distance of my trek sunk in. "What brought you all the way out here?"

"I needed a change of scenery, I guess. Ain't nothing good was coming out of that place for me, so I was either going to rot with the rest of them or I was going to get the heck out of dodge."

He licked his lips slowly, getting a spot of chocolate that was next to his piercing. "Well, I'm sure happy that you stumbled into our little town to make your fresh start."

"Yeah? Why?"

"Because that means I get to watch the caterpillar turn into a butterfly." He pointed to my collarbone where a bright purple butterfly was inked into my skin. "Don't worry. I'm not this sappy all the time."

With a wink he slurped on his milkshake as our meals were placed on the table. The rest of breakfast went on with light conversation as I picked at the huge omelet that was like another orgasm in my mouth. I could definitely get used to how good the food was in this town. To say the least, I'd freaked out for nothing. Abel was easygoing and sweet with a deep, gruff side that made my heart flutter and my panties wet every time his deep drawl cloaked over a sexual innuendo followed by him biting those sexy-as-hell lip rings.

"Well, your car does need a starter. I was hoping I was wrong, but oh well, it'll be taken care of." Abel sighed as he shoved his phone back into his front jeans pocket. "Did you have plans other than work for today?"

I shook my head, taking my seat on the back of his bike.

"Good, 'cause she isn't gonna be ready until the morning. One of my guys has to run to grab a part for it and I'll probably head that way tonight to make sure she's done right."

"I feel bad that I'm causing all this trouble." I rested my head on Abel's shoulder, way too intimate of a move for someone I had just met, but damn I was drawn to him.

"Wanna hang with me for a bit? I just have to grab

Raine from school in a few hours, but I can show you around town, maybe convince you to stick around while you're trying to find whatever it is you think you're missing in your life."

"Raine?" I asked as Abel guided my arms around his middle.

I could feel him take a deep breath in before he answered, "My daughter."

———

AFTER ABEL SHOWED me around the small town of Vilas, playing tour guide from the front of his bike, we made our way up a long gravel road off the side of a mountain.

"Where are you taking me now?"

We slowly pulled up a driveway to a large two-story old farmhouse without a neighbor in sight. Abel hit the kickstand and let me get off the bike.

"We gotta get Raine here in a few minutes so I needed to stop in and grab my truck."

It took me by surprise that he wanted me to go with him to get his daughter from school. "Abel, you can just take me back to the motel. You don't have to—"

He held his hand up, cutting me off while he shook his head. "You're going to love her and she'll get a kick out of being around another girl for once."

I could feel curiosity starting to get the better of me

about why Raine's mother wasn't in the picture and why there wasn't a ring on this gorgeous man's finger, but I left it alone. If he wanted me to know what happened to her, he would tell me.

He grabbed my hand and a chill raced from my fingertips to my pussy, which immediately woke up and begged to say a very intimate hello to Abel. He led me over to a brand new lifted Ford F250 and my panties soaked on the spot.

"That's one gorgeous truck." I blushed as his hand got tighter.

"Like trucks, do ya Crickett?"

I bit my lip and nodded. There was no way in hell that this guy could get any sexier.

The eyes.

The piercings on his lip.

The sleeve of tattoos that covered his hard-as-heck muscles.

The slow, deep drawl.

The bike, the boots, the truck. The soft side that bit back under his tough as nails exterior.

I was fucking infatuated in one fell swoop, right as our lips touched as he pressed me up against the shiny white paint of his Ford. His fingers gripped my hipbones as a low moan escaped my throat. Slowly our tongues met as his soft lips parted mine. By the end I was practically gasping for the breath he had taken away from me.

I sighed, leaning into his chest as he rested his chin on the top of my head. "There's something so perfect about you, Crickett."

I pulled away from him, locking eyes with his smoldering ocean gaze. "You don't even know me."

"I have never wanted anything more than to know you." He kissed my forehead. "C'mon. I don't want to keep Raine waiting."

We hopped into the truck and within minutes we were pulling into the elementary school pickup line. A little blonde ball of energy raced for the truck once it caught her eye. She shoved a flower she had just picked into her bright pink backpack.

Abel jumped out of the driver's seat, scooping the running girl into his large arms. He swallowed her up tight into his chest, placing kisses all over her giggling face. Once he got her buckled into the backseat, he pointed up to me.

"Raine, I want you to meet a new friend of mine."

She waved and bounced in her seat. "Hi! What's your name?"

I waved, holding back the giddiness that fluttered in my chest after watching such a tough guy melt into a puddle of mushy gushy feelings and love once his daughter was in his arms.

"It's very nice to meet you Raine, I'm Crickett."

She giggled. "I like that name."

"Yeah? Thanks. I like yours a lot, too."

"Want to see Miss Gilda?" She chirped while digging through her bag.

"Sure."

She victoriously held up a little unicorn-looking rubber ducky with a rainbow tail and mane.

"She's so pretty!" I exclaimed as Raine smiled wide, holding her little plastic friend to her chest.

"Thanks." Raine beamed, still bouncing in her seat. "Here." She grabbed the flower out of her bag. "This is for you."

I choked from the flood of feels that rushed over me as I took the white daisy from the little girl's hand. "That is so pretty. Thank you, Raine. We'll put it in water when we get you home."

Abel grabbed my hand, mouthing, "Thank you."

I mouthed back, "Of course," squeezing his hand back.

"Crickett?" Raine called from the backseat.

"Yes?" I turned in my seat, resting my chin on the backrest.

"You're pretty. You should be my new mommy."

Fire burned my chest, neck, and cheeks as Abel choked and laughed from the front seat. Thankfully he saved me.

"Raine, honey, Crickett and I are just friends, but hopefully she'll be able to hang out with us a little bit while she's in town."

"Miss Gilda and I would really like that," she stated while bouncing the rubber toy on her knee and looking out the window.

When we got back to Abel's house, Raine showed me her pretty pink princess room with all of her dolls and toys. She and I played for hours, coloring and playing Barbies, marrying Ken and Barbie—Barbie even rode into her wedding on the back of Miss Gilda. Abel left us to go to the garage to help the guys with my car for a while, and I was kind of glad to have a little one-on-one time with Raine. She was such a sparkling light that my spirits were lifted right away and I felt like I had been in this little girl's life for years, not just hours.

Before I knew it, Abel was calling up to both of us that dinner was ready. Talk about time freaking flying by. It was so wonderful to spend an afternoon completely care-free with a child that was so sweet and innocent.

We ate pizza while Raine chattered away with her dad about her day at school and told him all about how much fun we'd had playing together.

"All right, you little princess. It's time for a bath and then off to bed with you."

She crossed her arms and gave him puppy dog eyes. "But I'm not..." She took in a deep breath as a yawn escaped. "Slllleeeeeppppyyy..."

Abel let out a soft laugh, lifting her into his arms.

"How about you go take a bath and then Crickett can read you a story before bed?"

He looked up at me to make sure that was ok. I smiled and gave him a quick nod. "That sounds like fun, Raine. Besides, doesn't Miss Gilda need a bath too? She played a whole lot today."

She shrugged. "Yeah. Ok."

With her dad's pinky in her hand, they marched up the stairs to the bath.

"There's beer in the fridge, this won't take long. Make yourself at home."

I grabbed a cup of water and watched a Friends rerun while I waited for my cue to head up for story time. My heart felt so full of love and emotion seeing such a loving father with his daughter. I knew there had been times like that with my dad, but most of those memories had been lost along the way.

I could tell that Abel and Raine weren't the only ones that lived in this huge house. It was a total dude's house too, except for the explosion of pinkish-purples in Raine's room. The walls barely had art on them, there was mostly beer in the fridge—other than stuff for Raine —and the smell of bachelor pad emanated from every room. I hoped that none of them came through the door to find me on the couch by myself in their home.

CHAPTER 5

After reading the first half of <u>Beauty and the Beast</u>, Raine dozed off in my arms.

"Did she fall asleep quick?" Abel asked from the couch in the living room as I grabbed a beer from the fridge.

Taking a seat next to him, I nodded. "She's precious."

"She's pretty amazing for sure." He wrapped his arm around me, pulling me into his rock hard chest.

"I'll take you to get your car in the morning." He kissed the top of my head. "I can take you back to the motel now though, if you want."

There was not a snowball's chance in hell that I wanted to go back to the motel and leave his arms, but my brain was telling me that I still didn't know this guy and that I should have my guard and high ass walls up to protect myself.

"I don't want to go. Today has been more perfect than I can really explain."

"What hurt you so badly, babe? Why are you running from something?"

I sighed into him. "I don't know if I should put it into words or just let all the bad memories die in the past where they belong."

Abel pulled me onto his lap. "We all got some skeletons, Crickett. As long as we don't let them define us then we can move on. Stop letting them have a hold on you. Don't let them win."

"We just met, but I feel like I was supposed to come here."

He hugged me to him. "Good, because I knew the moment I saw you and those bright red lips of yours that you were sent here for me to know."

It was so cliché but right then, he grabbed a fistful of my hair and pulled me in for another show-stopping kiss. My body buzzed just from our lips connecting. It was freaking incredible.

I pulled away from him. "Maybe we shouldn't." I bit my lip. It was better to at least try to be hard to get, even if my lady parts were screaming for him.

"I can make up the couch for you or take you back. It's up to you." He leaned down and kissed right under my ear, whispering softly, "Or I have a very comfortable bed upstairs. We can just sleep. I can be a gentleman when I have to be."

I nodded, getting up from his lap. "Yeah. Ok."

We made our way up to his room, on the opposite side of the house from Raine's, which made me feel way more comfortable. If I was going to sleep with her father, I didn't want her to hear us.

"Here." Abel handed me a faded AC/DC shirt and a pair of basketball shorts. "You can sleep in these. The bathroom is there if you want to change with some privacy."

"Where did you come from?" I laughed quietly, taking the clothes and heading to the bathroom.

"What?" He smiled his killer panty-dropping smile while pulling his cut and shirt off and tossing them on the armchair in the corner of the room.

"You're just like a freaking Prince Charming swooping in to save the damsel." I had to take a minute to catch my breath as I gaped at his chiseled abs and rock hard tattooed chest. I hadn't thought it was possible for him to be any hotter than what I had pictured, but right there he was proving me wrong. The words "respect few, fear none" were etched into his skin with a badass skull in the middle. I was a total sucker for a guy with sexy tattoos.

He took a few steps toward me, then put his hands on

my hips. His eyes were soft and deep as he looked into mine. "I'll be Prince Charming if you need one, but trust me, this prince has a rough side to him. It's just...for some reason you don't bring out that part of me. Maybe later." He winked and quickly smacked my ass. "Now get changed. I'm fucking exhausted."

His hand hitting my ass made my sex clench and my heart start racing. I wanted him more than ever right then. The image of just pouncing on him was all too tempting, but I really wanted to take things slower than I had so far. I was already about to climb into bed with the guy, maybe I shouldn't give all the milk away for free within the first few days of knowing him.

We climbed into bed and within ten minutes we were both sound asleep. I had a peaceful night full of steamy flashes of everything I wanted Abel to do to me, from deep sensual kisses all the way to tying me to his bed and coming on my face, with so many more fun adventures in between.

I was slowly brought out of my dream-filled sleep by Abel wrapping his arms around me and kissing my neck.

"Morning." I yawned, rolling in his arms to look into his sleepy eyes.

"Mornin' sugar."

I gently kissed his lips. "What time is it?"

There was barely any light coming in from the window; it had to be the ass crack of dawn.

"Just about five-thirty. Raine wakes up around seven so I try to be up before her when I have someone over."

The thought of Abel sharing his bed with other women wasn't a crazy notion—he was a fucking dude—but jealously and possession washed over me in an instant. It was completely irrational but I hated the thought of him even touching other women.

"Does that mean I have to leave?" I couldn't hide the disappointment in my voice as I sat up in the king size bed, wrapped in Abel's amazingly soft sheets.

"No, that's not what I meant. I just don't want her to run in here and find me in bed with a chick. I like to be up and moving around so she doesn't get the wrong idea." He pulled me down, back into his arms. "I don't know how to raise a kid, I'm going in blind here. I'm just trying to do the best that I can."

I nodded and kissed his stubbly cheek. "I totally get it."

"You know you're the first chick I have let meet Raine since her mom died."

Bam. That bomb had just been dropped. Raine's mom was freaking dead and he just let it roll off his tongue like it was yesterday's news. I was stunned. I had no idea what to say.

"Wow. I'm sorry."

His grip on me tightened. "It's been a while. It's hard but we're moving on."

"Do you want to talk about it?"

He shook his head. "Maybe later. I don't want to spoil what's left of this morning with a sad trip down memory lane." I watched his bare tattooed chest inflate as he sucked in a deep breath before he pulled me on top of him to straddle his waist.

I leaned over and kissed him. "I don't know why I am this comfortable with you. It kind of scares the shit out of me."

"I think I am going to take that as a compliment." His husky voice was thick with lust dripping from it as he laced his fingers in my hair and guided my lips to his.

Slowly our bodies went into a hyper drive of passion. Our lips moved together as my heart started racing and his grip on my messy hair got tighter. I could feel his need for me grow as I gradually started to grind my swelling bud onto him through our clothes. I completely threw all notions of taking things slow with my beautiful stranger out the window. There was no turning back at that point.

I yanked his shirt off over my head and it was like a light switch went off in Abel's mind. Through gritted teeth he sucked in a sharp breath and let out a lust filled moan as he gently pushed me onto the bed. He gripped the waistband of the basketball shorts I was wearing and looked me dead in the eyes. His gaze was almost black as he licked his pierced lip slowly.

"I want you, Crickett. Right the fuck now. If you want

me to stop this is your only fucking chance." His voice was strong, possessive. His chest heaved as he waited for my response.

"Abel, I want you. I've never wanted a man more."

He looked up and down my body while he hesitated again. "Just know, you'll be mine. In this moment I will claim you."

His words should have sent me running. That should have been a red flag and I should have been scared of him and what they truly meant, but I was so consumed by him and the power over me he lusted for. It was one of the most intoxicating moments of my life. I had never wanted anything more than to be his, only his.

"Do I have to say it again?"

He nodded.

"Take me, Abel."

He growled softly. "Say you're mine, Crickett."

"I'm all yours, Abel."

With that he yanked off the shorts and his boxer briefs. His erect member was one of the most gorgeous dicks I had ever seen and definitely the biggest.

I licked my lips. "Let me taste you."

A fire lit in his eyes. He grabbed my shoulders, pulled me down so my head was off the pillow, and straddled my head.

"If it gets too intense, just grab my thigh hard. Ok?"

I nodded and licked the tip of his dick slowly. "I think I can handle you, babe."

A deep chuckle came from down in his chest. "I hope so, sugar, because I am not the most gentle man to say the least. Now open your fucking mouth."

I'd had guys attempt dirty talk in the past, but none of them were ever good at it or really meant their words. With Abel, he was in charge and meant every command that leapt from his desire filled throat, and nothing had ever turned me on more. I felt slickness pool as my clit throbbed from the feeling of him slamming his cock into the back of my throat.

I sucked and licked while he thrust in and out of my mouth roughly. Tears formed in the corners of my eyes as he pushed harder with each thrust.

"Fuck, Crickett. You're so goddamn good at this."

I felt my sex ache for him. Want was building fast as I gripped his thigh.

Immediately he pulled away. "Are you ok?"

The amount of concern he showed was comforting. "Yeah. I want you to fuck me."

His lips pulled into a sensual smile as he rolled me back on top of him. "As you wish, babe. But I want to see those tits bounce as your cunt takes in my dick."

Fucking chills.

Goosebumps coursed up and down my entire body as he pressed his thumb to my clit, slowly teasing me.

"Condom?"

Panting, Abel pointed to the nightstand. "Top drawer."

I leaned over and yanked that drawer open as fast as I could while my knees were shaking from the small circles he continued to draw on my slick folds. Shoving my hand in, I felt what I thought was a condom wrapper, but what did I find instead? Fun Dip.

"Really?" I couldn't help the laugh that flew out as I threw the blue package of my favorite childhood candy onto Abel's bare muscular chest.

He shrugged. "So I have a sweet tooth, doesn't everyone?"

I nodded, grabbing the candy. "I know what I'm having for dessert after."

"You'll need it once I am done with you."

Abel rolled me off of him, grabbed a condom, and ripped the foil with his teeth. He handed it to me. "Go nice and slow, babe. Let's make an event out of this."

I climbed on top of him, doing as he asked, taking my time rolling the condom over him. He sucked in a sharp breath, gripping my hips tightly.

"Take it in."

I rubbed the head of his dick over my slick lips, smirking a little. His grip got tighter, his jaw working intensely as he watched me.

"Don't be a damn tease, babe," he growled. He was not amused with my playtime.

"Fine." I leaned back, positioning him at my opening. "How badly do you want it?"

"I think how hard my fucking dick is speaks for itself you firecracker." He slapped my ass hard, gripping it firmly with one hand. "Fuck me, Crickett."

I took my time taking him in. I gasped as I felt myself stretching, letting him consume me.

"Oh my God." I moaned and started to rock my hips, grinding softly into him.

"Your cunt is so damn tight. Holy fucking shit."

With his hand still on my ass, he pushed me hard down onto him, bucking his hips up into mine. He was perfectly positioned and within minutes I felt my climax building quickly in the pit of my stomach.

"I'm going to fucking come," I moaned into his ear as I dug my nails into his shoulders.

"Not yet." He pulled out and rolled me onto my stomach. "Lean on your forearms and get that cunt in the fucking air, sugar."

"I've never..." I blushed before I finished my statement. I wasn't used to many positions. I wasn't really well-versed in sex at all, except what I'd learned watching porn alone with my battery powered pocket boyfriend. I had been with a few people but they'd all sucked or were lazy assholes. The trailer park didn't have too many options in the men department and there was no freaking way I was going to sleep with one of the customers at the strip club. That was more my mom's style, not mine.

"There's a first for everything, babe. This will be fun. I like being your first for something."

He guided me into the position, kneeling behind me and wrapping his hands around my waist. Pulling me close to him, he leaned down and kissed my back. "This might hurt at first. Play through the pain. It will be worth it."

Pain quickly crashed with pleasure as he plunged into me. My knees shook as I gripped the comforter under me. It was the first time I had felt this much pleasure from sex, ever. Period. Hands down. I was quickly addicted.

He pressed his thumbs harder into the small of my back, pulling me firmly into him and making me cry out.

"Like that, Crickett?"

"More than you know!" I groaned into the blanket.

He thrust into me faster and harder, pulling my hips back into him as his balls smacked against my swollen clit. I cried out without even realizing what I was doing. Quickly, he wrapped his hand around my mouth.

"Shhh." He whispered, "You'll wake up the whole freaking house, babe."

I forced my voice to level. "I'm so close, Abel."

"Good." His gravely tone sent electricity up my spine. "I'm going to come with you."

Our bodies shook and pulsed as our climaxes crashed around us.

I felt drunk, at least that was the closest feeling I could compare to how amazing I felt in that moment.

Abel pulled me to him and kissed right under my ear. "You're perfect."

"You're pretty unbelievable yourself."

"Let's get cleaned up. Raine is going to be getting up soon."

Abel shoved up from the bed, making his way into the bathroom. I heard the shower start and I hoped he wouldn't mind if I hopped in with him. My body craved to be near his, even though it had been only seconds since he'd walked away; it was more than a little unnerving, but also thrilling all at once. I had never lusted before. Maybe I had never really liked a man more than just a little crush. Whatever was going on with me, my head, and my libido, for the first time in my life I was going with the flow and enjoying myself, not worrying about what my next move had to be. It was pretty incredible.

A pounding sounded on the door and I quickly covered myself with the sheet.

Abel ran to the door with a towel wrapped around his waist and threw it open. "What the fuck?"

Holt was standing in the doorway. "It's Rave, he didn't

check in after his meeting in Riverside last night and no one can get ahold of him."

Rave. That name sent chills through me again. *Could it really be my dad? How many Raves existed in the world?* My body started shaking as I pulled the covers higher up my chest.

"Fuck. Yeah, ok." Abel rubbed the back of his neck. "Let me get some damn clothes on and I'll be down in a second."

Holt nodded and turned to leave, but not before peeking around Abel to wave at me.

Well this is humiliating.

Abel slammed the door, grumbling to himself.

"Can I help?" I started to pull my jeans on.

"Actually, how comfortable are you with driving trucks?"

I shrugged. "Friends back home used to let me take their mud trucks out all the time. Why?"

"Would you mind taking Raine to school and maybe picking her up? I really need to handle this right away."

"I don't mind at all. What should I do about work?"

Abel shook his head. "I'll handle that. While I'm gone, you won't have to work."

He grabbed a piece of paper from his dresser, scribbled on it, and handed it to me. "Here is the number of the house I will be staying at while I am away, just in case I don't have cell service. Call if you need anything. Drive my truck around, we'll grab your car when I get back into town. I don't want to worry about you getting stranded again."

He threw clothes on, shoved his keys into his pocket, kissed me on the forehead, and headed out the door. "I'll check in with you guys tonight." He called through the door before jogging down the stairs.

I hopped in the shower for a quick rinse off, rummaged through his shirts until I found one small enough to pass on me, and made my way down to the kitchen to make a pot of coffee.

Right as the pot was finishing up Raine bounced into the kitchen. "Where's Daddy?" she asked while climbing onto one of the big wooden chairs at the table I was leaning on.

Holt followed her in. "He had to go meet up with Pop, but he'll be back soon, sweetheart." He patted her on the head before grabbing two mugs out of the cupboard and handing one to me.

"Thanks."

He nodded. "Thanks for sticking around here to help with her. Don't worry about the bar, a few of the guys and Ronda are going to pick up some hours here and there. We'll be fine. Just do what you have to."

"Ronda's okay with that?"

I could just picture her freaking out when they called this early in the morning to add hours to her shifts.

Holt shrugged. "She's gonna have to be. Abel or Rich will deal with her. That ain't nothing for you to worry about."

"Sounds good to me, I guess." I shrugged before turning to Raine. "What do you want for breakfast, honey?"

"Captain Crunch, please." She sat at the table with Miss Gilda at her side while I fixed her a bowl of cereal.

CHAPTER 6

"How was school today, sweetie?"

Raine jumped into the front seat of Abel's truck, throwing her bag in the back seat. "It was ok."

She wasn't her normal, bouncing, bubbly self.

"What's up, gloomy? Everything all right?"

She shrugged. "Yeah." With a huge forced sigh she hugged Miss Gilda to her chest.

"Was someone mean to you today?"

She nodded.

"Was it a girl or boy?"

"It was a bunch of kids."

My heart gradually started breaking. No one ever deserved to be bullied, especially a child as sweet and goodhearted as Raine.

"What were they doing?"

She shifted in her seat, staring blankly out the window as I pulled out of the school's parking lot.

"It's ok, Raine. You can tell me."

"They were saying mean stuff at recess."

"Does this happen a lot?"

I kept glancing over at Raine as her cheeks got redder and redder, her nose started sniffling, and her eyes watered. I pulled the truck to the side of the road. I took my seatbelt off and shifted so I could put both my hands out for her to grab.

She just stared blankly at me. Clearly this was not something she felt comfortable telling grownups about. I really wished Abel was there to help handle it, but I couldn't let her be sad, it wasn't fair to her.

"Sweetie, please tell me. I know we just met, but I think we're really good friends. Good friends trust each other with big secrets. Would it make you feel better if I told you a secret first?"

She wiped her nose with her sleeve before nodding.

"Ok." I sighed and finally Raine took my hands, squeezing tightly. "I was bullied so bad in school because I didn't have a daddy. He had moved far away when I was just about your age. Kids were mean to me about it."

Her eyes got wide, like she was shocked someone else could relate to how mean kids could really be.

"Now can you tell me your secret?"

She took in a deep breath and with a sigh of relief, she whispered, "They were making fun of me because Mommy is in heaven."

I felt the waterworks welling quickly. Those freaking jerks at her school were little monsters. I wanted to turn that truck around and go spank each and every one of them and then tell their parents to put hot sauce on their tongues, or better yet soap like my mom used to do to me when I talked back to her.

"That's not fair sweetheart. I'm so sorry."

She forced a smile, gripping my hands with her tiny fingers. "It's ok. They don't have a mommy angel and I do."

And there ya had it: the most put together five-year-old on the freaking planet. Abel really was doing an amazing job with her.

"How about we get you home and we call your daddy to see if we can get some ice cream?"

She perked up in her seat. "Yay! Ice cream!"

Raine rushed into the house and got cleaned up as fast as she could while I called Abel.

His deep drawl came onto the line, sending chills down my arms instantly. "Hey, Crickett. Is everything ok?"

I started to pace in the kitchen. "Yeah, just got Raine home. She had a little bit of a rough day at school."

He sighed softly. "She's been having problems with a few of the kids in her class."

"She told me. Can I take her for ice cream tonight? Cheer her up a bit?"

I could hear the smile on his face. "After she does her homework, that sounds like a great idea."

"Awesome. How's everything goin'?" I had no idea if I could even ask about what was going on with the missing club member, I just wanted to know when he was going to be coming home without sounding needy or desperate.

"It's goin'. I'm gonna have to be out of town for a few more days than I expected. You don't mind staying at my place while I'm gone, do you? It's a huge help to Holt and me."

I didn't even have to think twice about it. "Sure. I can grab the rest of my stuff from the motel in the morning."

"Thanks babe. I have to run, I'll be in touch. Kiss Raine for me."

Holt ambled into the kitchen. "Was that Abel?" He asked, grabbing a beer from the fridge.

"Yes sir." I took a seat at the breakfast table.

Holt joined me. "Did he tell ya that he's going to be gone?"

I nodded. "I'm going to stick around here and help you with Raine. If that's okay with you."

"If that's what Abel asked you to do, that's fine by me.

We're swamped at the garage and short staffed at the bar. It's better if I'm there."

"Well, I'll hold down the fort. I really love Raine. She's awesome."

"I can agree to that. Oh, I forgot to tell you. I brought your car back so you don't have to keep driving that big ole truck around town, unless you want to."

"Thanks Holt, I appreciate it."

Raine came down the stairs and Holt left to veg out on the couch after a long day at work. After homework and some ramen noodles, I took Raine to get ice cream in town. She was completely carefree, not showing any signs of the hurt or frustration she'd had when leaving school only hours before. When we got back home it was bath time, and then I read Cinderella to her.

Right as her tired eyes started to flutter closed, she wrapped her tiny arms around my neck and kissed me on the cheek. "I'm glad you're here," she whispered, resting her head on my shoulder.

I kissed the top of her head. "So am I."

I shifted out from under her, pulling the covers up and making sure she was tucked in nice and tight.

"Goodnight, sweetie. Sleep well."

Climbing into Abel's massive bed not too long after tucking Raine in, with the soft cotton sheets and one of his soft white shirts and basketball shorts on, was amazing. I plugged my phone in on the nightstand, turned off the lights, and lay there wide-eyed. I knew I should have had a beer or two before bed to relax me a little but with being responsible for someone else's kid, I just didn't feel right about it.

I flipped through the late night channels trying to find something just boring enough to help put me to sleep. I finally settled on a documentary about cheetahs. The monotone voice of the narrator was as good as the Sandman throwing sleep in my eyes.

A few minutes later a text rattled my phone on the wooden table next to me.

Abel: Hope you're making yourself at home, babe. Wish I was there holding you.

Me: Your bed is a little lonely without you in it.

Abel: How's Raine doing?

Me: Fine. Much better than this afternoon.

Abel: Good. How are you doing?

Me: Can't sleep. You?

Abel: I wish I could help.

Me: You'll be home soon though.

Abel: I can't wait.

Me: Me either. I'm going to try to get some rest.

Abel: I have to be up early too. Kiss Raine for me.

Me: I will. Goodnight.

Abel: Night, sugar. Miss you.

Me: Miss you too.

CHAPTER 7

The next few days droned on. Since Abel was gone, Holt was working like a dog and Raine was in school, and most of the time I was bored out of my skull.

Right as I was closing Raine's door from putting her to sleep a little later than normal—it was Friday and I figured I could be a tad bit lenient since she didn't have to be up for school in the morning—I heard the front door slam and the sound of voices in the living room.

Nerves crashed into my stomach when Abel's gruff tone called up the stairs to me, "Babe? You here?"

I got freaking giddy as his boots started stomping up the stairs. "Yeah. Just put Raine down."

Her door swung open and she ran out. "Daddy!"

Abel scooped her into his arms. "Hey sugar. You should be in bed."

"I'm just so happy to see you!" She nuzzled and squeezed him and I saw his heart melt.

"Come on, let's get you back to bed."

"But you just got home. I want to spend time with you."

He kissed her cheek and laid her back down into her Tinkerbell covered bed. "We'll spend time together in the morning. Promise."

"Pinky promise?" She held her tiny pinky out for his.

"Pinky promise."

I was a puddle of goo on the floor watching how amazing he was with Raine. It made Abel that much sexier to me.

I followed Abel into his room.

"How'd everything go around here?" he asked while pulling his cut off. He threw it onto the chair and that's when I noticed the black eye and busted up knuckles.

"Fine." I tried to ignore it. I knew he probably wouldn't tell me what happened, why he was in a fight, but I guess I didn't do a good job of hiding the concern on my face.

Abel pulled a clean white shirt over his head before taking me into his arms. "Don't worry babe, it doesn't even hurt."

"Ok." That was all I could choke out before our lips were crashing together.

I gripped Abel's shirt, pulling him into me as he winced. "What?" I quickly pulled away from him.

"Just a bruised rib. Nothing to worry about."

"Did you at least find the guy you were looking for?"

He sat down on the bed, grabbing my hand to pull me over to him. "Yes. Everything has been taken care of and everyone is fine."

"That's good."

He nodded and scooped me into his arms, moving to carry me into the bathroom.

"What are you doing?" I giggled as he sat me down on the counter.

He kissed my hair before turning on the water in the shower. "I want to get cleaned up and I figured you should join me."

My hair was still damp from the shower I'd taken after dinner. "What if I don't want to?" I bit my lip as he walked over to me.

"I didn't ask, did I?"

The steam bellowed up over the glass door of the shower.

Before I knew what was happening, Abel had me in his arms, my back on the slick tile of the shower as the warm water rolled over our skin. He was gently nibbling my neck, sending chills down my body even in the warm water.

"God, I missed you." He rumbled in my ear, grabbing a fistful of my wet hair, pulling it back to extend my neck.

I moaned as the head of his cock rubbed my sensitive clit, making my want for him to fill me again grow.

"Are you on birth control?"

I hesitated. I was, but I had never been with a guy without a condom. I'd heard it was supposed to be so much better, but it scared me. I had no idea where his dick had been.

"Abel, I just don't think it's a good idea."

He sighed and set me down. He knelt and started to kiss my stomach.

I let his lips brush against my wet skin. "Have you ever had sex without a condom?"

"No. But I just don't know."

He pushed me against the wall with one hand and started rubbing his thumb over my bud. Gently he started to lick and suck my clit. My knees buckled from the gentle ecstasy as his tongue rolled over my delicate skin.

"Oh, my, God! Abel." I could barely stand as my knees shook. I gripped onto his muscular shoulders as he looked up at me. His eyes consumed me as the pleasure of that moment took over. Quickly my orgasm built in the pit of my stomach and crashed hard as my body shook and my hips bucked.

Abel got to his feet, kissing and nibbling on my hard nipples on his way back up.

"I can respect you not wanting to do it without a rubber, babe. You don't need to explain it. I'm clean. I'm assuming you are too and when you're ready I will fuck that pussy raw. I want to feel your skin on mine, but I can be patient."

He turned the shower off and handed me a towel.

"I'll be right back." He threw a towel around his dripping waist and left the bathroom. He returned quickly, dropping the towel on the floor. He slowly started to stroke his erection in his hand.

"Get on your hands and knees." He pointed down at the plush bathmat. His eyes smoldered as he watched me do as I was instructed.

The drop of pre-come released, so I slowly rolled my tongue over the soft head as his fingers laced in my hair. "Open."

I opened my mouth as he pushed into the back of my throat so hard I choked. It was surprisingly exhilarating.

"God, I love fucking your mouth." Abel moaned, thrusting faster and as hard as he could. I moaned too, my back arching from the pleasure of pleasing him.

He slid his dick out and pushed my head down onto the rug, slapping my ass. I heard him rip the condom wrapper. "I've wanted this since I had to run out of here the other morning. I have dreamed about your perfect ass and beautiful cunt. Say you're mine, Crickett."

I moaned into the rug. "Abel, I'm yours. Please shove your cock into my pussy."

His thumb rolled over my clit as his teeth nipped at my ass cheek. He slowly plunged his thumb into my wetness as he pushed my ass higher into the air.

I groaned and pulled away from him, rolling over onto my back. He pulled my hips up into his as he thrust into me and my world started spinning. It was so much fucking better than anything I had ever felt. He started off slow and gentle, building momentum.

"Your tits are so fucking sexy, bouncing as I push my dick into you."

I rolled my fingers over my hard sensitive nipples. Abel bit his piercing.

"Does that feel good babe?"

I nodded, my breath hitching as his nails dug into my hips.

"How about this?" He grabbed my other hand, taking my first two fingers and guiding them over my clit. My body shook uncontrollably as instantly an orgasm erupted.

"Holy fucking shit."

Abel smiled. "I'll take that as it was good too. My turn."

Without taking his dick out of my pussy, he picked me up and pressed me against the wall.

"That was impressive."

He bit my neck. "Sugar, you haven't seen anything yet. The things that I have planned to do to you will rock your world."

It only took a few fast, hard pumps before I felt Abel swell and pulse inside me as his head fell to my shoulder.

Abel carried me to the bed, climbing in next to me. He grabbed two packets of Fun Dip from the nightstand and glanced at me with a small smirk and a raised eyebrow.

"That looks freaking delicious."

He threw a blue raspberry over to me and we cuddled, eating candy like high schoolers after prom.

My eyes wandered over his bare chest, noticing the deep blues and purples covering his ribs.

"Do they hurt?"

He shook his head, licking the last of the blue powder off of the white candy stick. "Babe, there ain't nothin' to worry about." He kissed the top of my head. "I'm fine."

We threw away our empty rappers, Abel wrapping me up in his strong arms.

"Goodnight," he whispered.

———

WAKING up still cradled in Abel's arms in the middle of

the night was a little awkward. The whole thing was awkward, but perfect in its own way. How do two people just fall into such a great rhythm like that so fast? It felt like Abel and I were two puzzle pieces that had finally found each other.

I wiggled out from under his arm, pulled his shirt on over my bare body, and made my way down to the kitchen, praying for a cold bottle of water.

I opened up the fridge to find one last bottle. I cracked the seal and started to chug when I was startled out of my skin by a raspy voice coming from the kitchen table.

"Who the heck are you?" asked the mysterious stranger cloaked in the shadows. I shot around to look at him, gasping for breath and nearly spitting all the water out onto myself.

I flipped on the kitchen light and my heart sank. It was like I was looking directly into my own eyes.

I started hyperventilating.

I was dizzy.

My entire body started shaking.

"Crickett? Is that you?" the man said, getting up from the table.

"What the fuck are you doing here?" I spit out, stepping backward into the refrigerator as I recoiled from the man that used to be my dad.

"I should be asking you the same question."

Abel's large frame took up the entryway to the kitchen. "Rave? Crickett? Everything okay in here?"

"So it really is you!" Rave's eyes got wide, staring at me.

"Do you know her, Dad?"

I couldn't breathe. "Did you just call him..." I was about to pass the fuck out.

No fucking way.

This cannot be happening.

"Abel is my stepson." Rave took his seat again at the table with a sigh. "And this young lady over here is my daughter."

Abel's face got white. He started to pace the floor. "Is he why you came to this town?"

I nodded.

"You've been looking for me?" Rave pulled the chair out next to him, but there was no way I could be that close to him yet. I was too freaked out, not to mention I was practically naked, standing there in just a white t-shirt. Thankfully Abel was so much bigger than me that his shirt was like a damn dress, but still, I had never felt more exposed in my life, especially with both of them staring at me.

I had imagined seeing my father again over and over for years, but I'd never thought that he'd be sitting in the kitchen in a motorcycle gang vice president's house wearing a matching cut at four in the freaking morning claiming to be his goddamn stepfather. This was all too damn much for me to take.

"Fuck you, Rave!" I yelled and stormed out of the kitchen and straight out the front door, grabbing my purse and keys off the coffee table on my way.

"Crickett wait!" I could hear Rave running after me.

Tears were already pouring down my face as I ran down the front steps off the porch.

"Please let me explain," he called after me, but I was already in my car, engine going.

I rolled down my window. "You had your chance to explain for years. Instead you ran up the mountain and played dad for another fucking kid? You make me sick."

I sped out of the driveway and was just about a mile down the road when I realized that I had no idea where to go. I still had the motel room, but the key for it was back at Abel's, along with all my other shit.

I really need to start thinking things through more often.

Quickly the headlights of two motorcycles were hot on my tail. Abel rode up next to me and started yelling at me to pull over. I was crying hysterically, shaking my head no and swerving all over the road.

All of a sudden, Rave was in front of me, braking. I swerved off the road, barely missing his back bumper, and slammed my car in park.

I was a mess. My emotions were getting the better of me.

Snot was pouring from my nose.

I wasn't wearing real clothes.

I wanted to be mad, but I was more hurt than anything.

Abel got off his bike and came to my window. "Crickett," he yelled through the window, "Unlock your doors now."

I shook my head, hands glued to the steering wheel.

"I'm not asking. Let me in this goddamn car. You're too upset to be driving. You'll fucking kill yourself or worse, someone else."

There was no one on the roads at four in the morning in this tiny town in the mountains of North Carolina, but I knew he was right: I was too upset to be driving. I slid over into the passenger seat and hit the unlock button. Abel slid into the driver's side and locked the car again. He grabbed my hand.

"So Rave's your old man, huh?"

I nodded.

Thanks Captain Obvious.

"That doesn't change the way I feel about you." He was firm, resolute.

I stared out the window at Rave as he just sat on his bike with his head in his hands. "I don't know if I can do this."

"Do what? See him or be with me?"

"Both, maybe. Fuck, I don't know. I just fucked my goddamned stepbrother." The words made me feel sick.

Abel started laughing a little.

I shot him an evil eye, tears still staining my face. "What the fuck could be so funny right now?"

"Have you seen Joe Dirt?"

I nodded.

"The scene where he's fucking that chick that isn't his sister but he makes her scream 'I'm your sister' just popped into my head."

I gasped and slammed my fist into this shoulder. "You're an ass."

"Yeah, probably." He grabbed my hand. "Look. We're two freaking adults. An hour ago we were the same two fucking people as we are right now. Just because you're Rave's daughter, you think that changes?"

I shrugged. "It's just all so fucked."

His lips brushed the back of my hand. "Rave married my mom after I was eighteen. I only call him Dad since I don't have one anymore and it's less confusing for Raine."

Abel's eyes filled with pain and the ice that had built up around my heart in the last thirty minutes started to melt.

"Is he good to her?"

"The best. I don't have any family left. I have the club and Rave. That's it."

"Daddy! Higher!"

The warm sun beat down on my smiling face as my dad pushed me higher and higher on the swing. It was a beautiful warm summer day.

"How's that princess?"

He shoved me harder and I went flying through the air as fast as the wind.

"Weeee!" I screamed.

"Let's get you home for some lunch." He grabbed the swing to slow it down.

"Just a little bit longer?" I pleaded, popping out my lower lip.

He grabbed me, holding me close to his chest as he kissed my cheek. "Tomorrow's your first day of school, don't you want to get your Cinderella backpack all ready?"

I gasped with excitement. "Yeah!"

"Ok, well then we better head home. Love you princess."

He kissed my hair and walked us over to his white truck. "Love you too, Daddy!"

Tears were streaming down my face as Abel shook my shoulder. "Zone out there for a minute, babe?"

Ugh. Hearing my stepbrother call me babe was weird, but not even an hour before he'd been my beautiful stranger that I was falling hard and fast for.

This is going to take some getting used to.

At the end of the day, he was mine and I was his, even though it was wrong. I barely knew him; he was my boss, not to mention my freaking stepbrother. It just felt too right.

I mumbled, "Yeah. Just remembering."

"Good stuff?"

That's when I realized I was smiling, still looking out the window to Rave, who looked extremely distraught.

"He loved me."

I had finally remembered how much he had meant to me and I him. We really did have a bond, and that made it that much more confusing.

"Why didn't he fight for me?"

"I think Rave is the only one that will be able to answer that one."

I slumped down in my seat. "Can you take me home?"

"Of course, as long as by home, you mean back to my place so you can get some pants on and finally get the answers you've been looking for."

"Thanks." I leaned over and kissed Abel's stubble covered cheek.

Abel dialed Holt. "Hey man, sorry to wake you."

I felt terrible that Holt had to keep cleaning up my messes.

"I need you to come with me to pick up my bike in a minute. I'm driving Crickett back to the house in her car. Long story. Get dressed. Be home in a minute."

CHAPTER 8

After getting back to Abel's house, putting clothes on, and pacing around Abel's room nervously for about thirty minutes trying to talk myself out of my next move, I went down to the kitchen where Abel and Rave were sitting at the dining room table.

Abel shoved up from the table when he saw me making my way into the room. "Well, I'll leave you two to it for a bit. I'll be right upstairs if you need me." He squeezed my shoulder before heading up the stairs.

Words escaped me as I took the seat across the table from my father. I crossed my arms; my heart was guarded and I was completely prepared to keep those high ass walls in place.

He cleared his throat. "Do you have questions for me?"

I shrugged. I had a million, but I had no idea where to start. I felt all of my walls growing higher with reinforced steel being added.

He shifted in his seat, went and grabbed two beers from the fridge, opened them, and set one down in front of me with a koozie on it already.

I smirked a little. "That's the only way to really drink a beer."

He took a sip. "Ah, yup. Nice and cold with a koozie on it. You don't want cold hands or warm beer."

I laughed to myself, thumbing the tab on the top of the can. "I say that too."

A little bit of the tension melted away as we sat in silence for a few minutes.

Finally, Rave's gruff voice broke the quiet. "How'd you know to find me here?"

I looked into his eyes for the first time since I'd realized it was really him. "I got a letter from you when I was ten. The return address said Vilas."

"You got one of my letters?" He perked up a little, shifting an old shoebox in front of him.

"One of? I only got one ever. Didn't feel like writing to your kid was too important did you?"

The crow's feet at the corners of his eyes pulled down as concern spread across his face. "I wrote you hundreds of letters over the years. Here, let me show you."

He walked the large box over to my end of the table and took the seat next to mine. "They always got returned to me, but I kept trying. I'm glad one got through."

I opened the shoebox to see letter after letter unopened, some looking only weeks old, all with my mother's chicken scratch on it: *Wrong address. Return to sender.*

My heart hurt.

"How could she?" My voice shook as tears stung my eyes.

Rave sat quietly as I tore through the box, getting down to what looked like files of legal papers dating up until my sixteenth birthday.

"You fought for me?"

His head fell as tears started to drip slowly down his cheeks. "There wasn't much I could do after your mom claimed I beat her that night I ran off. I got about thirty minutes down the road before cops were cuffing me and throwing me in jail for three days. There's so much to tell you, sweetheart. But please just know that the moral of all this is I never wanted to leave you with her. I wanted to protect you and I failed."

"I was so wrong all these years." My head was spinning, trying to take it all in.

His hand landed on mine and I laced my fingers through his, gripping with all my might.

"All those years wasted." He coughed a little. "And look at you." He tried to smile. "You've turned into such a beautiful woman. Abel is quite taken with you, and that says a lot."

I wiped the tears from my cheeks. "So what now?"

He leaned back in his chair. "We make up for lost time."

———

WE SAT and talked for hours, about the good and the bad. He told me how he'd actually been part of another chapter of the Unacceptables back in Arkansas and that was how he'd found his way to North Carolina. I went on to tell him about how my mother had spiraled out of control. I even told him that I used to be a stripper. I could tell the words stung, but he listened and didn't show judgement.

When I heard Raine's light footsteps trotting down the stairs, I felt like no time had passed with my father and me.

Raine bolted for him. "Pop!" she yelled, jumping into his arms. "Have you met my friend Crickett yet?"

He smiled and kissed her forehead. "Yes, we're

becoming fast friends too." He winked at me as she bounced Miss Gilda on the table.

"Good. We need to keep her around. She's pretty and nice. I like that." She beamed at me and grabbed my hand. "Will you make me Captain Crunch again? You do it the best with the perfect amount of milk."

Raine started dragging me into the kitchen and I glanced over to Rave. "Thank you." I breathed as relief flooded me. It wasn't the scenario I had pictured for all those years, but slowly I was realizing that the situation I had stumbled into was probably better.

He pursed his lips slowly as he nodded. "See you later. I need to head in to the shop."

Abel made his way down the stairs, catching Rave at the front door. I strained to eavesdrop on their conversation as I grabbed the fixings for Raine's breakfast.

"How'd it go?" Abel's hands were dug deep into his packets as he glared at Rave.

"Better than I expected."

Abel's shoulders relaxed. "Good. Heading down to the garage?"

Rave nodded and Abel slapped him on the back. "I should be heading up there in a few hours, we'll see how the day goes. Tell Ronda to cover Crickett's shift again this morning."

"Will do." With that Rave was out the door and I was happily sipping coffee at the breakfast table while Raine chattered away about how happy she was that it was Saturday and she didn't have to go to school.

Abel poured himself a cup of coffee and topped off my mug, even adding in a little extra sugar for me. "Hey, Raine?"

She looked up at him with wide eyes, chomping on a mouthful of cereal. "Yeah, Daddy?" I laughed as milk spilled down her chin while she spoke.

"How about Crickett and I take you to the park over on Elm today?"

She perked up in her seat and started bouncing as her cheeks got red. "That's the one with the really big slide!" The excitement that was pouring out of her was intoxicating.

"It sure is. Finish your breakfast and brush your teeth."

Raine scarfed down the rest of her food and bolted up the stairs to get ready. I rinsed my mug with her bowl and started to load the dishwasher when I felt Abel's hands run up my arms.

He gently kissed the top of my head. "Are we ok?"

I turned into his arms, wrapping mine around his waist. "Yes." Our lips slowly brushed together for the faintest touch of a kiss. "Sorry I freaked out last night."

He chuckled a little, pulling away to dig his cigarette box out of his jeans pocket. "You're not the only one that was freaking out. I thought I was losing you right when I finally had you."

I rested my cheek on his warm, bare chest. "You're not getting rid of me that easily."

He let out a slow sigh. "Good."

"Am I ever going to be able to work again?" I questioned, pulling away from him to close the dishwasher. "My boss might get pissed if I keep missing shifts like this."

He lightly smacked me on my ass before putting a cigarette between his teeth. "I think he can handle it." With a wink he started to head for the front porch. "Want to join me?"

I followed him out onto the massive front porch, taking the lit cigarette from him before he lit his own.

"She's really taking to you." Abel motioned toward the front door.

We leaned against the railing, Abel's arm wrapping around my shoulders. "I'm taking to her like a bee to honey. You got one freaking amazing kid there."

His lips dusted the top of my ear. "You're freaking amazing."

I couldn't help but laugh. "You're insane."

"How do you figure?" Abel shifted to look at me as smoke blew out from the corner of his mouth.

"I'm a fucking basket case. I ran away from home to find a man that I can barely remember and wound up here in the middle of family drama and an MC. Pretty nuts, if I do say so myself."

"Don't you believe in fate?" His blue eyes were soft as he laced our fingers together.

"Don't start getting all soft and mushy on me, Abel Hellock. Aren't you supposed to be some sort of badass?"

He laughed a little. "Yeah, something like that." He threw his half smoked cigarette on the floor and stomped it out. "Let me go throw a shirt on, Raine will freak if I'm not ready when she is."

Right then she came clambering down the stairs, swinging open the front door. "Daddy! Get ready! Miss Gilda and I want to scream down the slide again."

Abel tossed me the keys to his truck. "Start her up for me? I'll be down in a minute."

Spending the better part of the late morning and early afternoon at the park with Raine and Abel was the perfect lighthearted fun I needed to relax from the night before. We all ran, swung, slid, twirled, and screamed until Raine was begging for pizza and ice cream.

"One or the other," Abel teased, carrying Raine back to the truck.

"Fine! Pizza."

I hopped into the passenger seat and Abel made the throaty diesel engine groan to life.

He grabbed my hand, a huge grin plastered on his face. "How does pizza sound to you?"

I glanced back at Raine as she buckled the seatbelt. "I think it sounds like a delicious idea!"

"Yay!" Raine cheered from the backseat.

We got a large pie delivered to the house and after we ate, I put Raine down for a nap.

Abel was sitting on the couch with two glasses of whiskey on the rocks resting on the coffee table.

"Double fisting?"

He glanced up at me from the box of Rave's letters and paperwork that was sitting open. "I figured you might need a stiff drink after I saw all this."

I sighed and sunk into the couch next to him. "Thanks. You couldn't be more right."

I took a nice slow sip, letting the amber liquid coat my throat.

"Weren't you supposed to head into work at some point today?" I propped my feet up on the coffee table and threw a blanket over my lap.

"Yeah, but this was way more fun. Sometimes you just need to play hooky."

I didn't know how to ask what I wanted to, but I needed to know. "Abel?"

"Yeah babe?"

I stalled, rubbing my thumb over the edge of my glass, staring at the amber liquid swirling around the ice. "What happened to Raine's mom and yours?" I finally spit out.

"Crickett, it's just hard to talk about." His eyes glassed

over and his finger ran around the rim of his glass as he evaded the growing elephant in the room.

I grabbed his hand. The contact caught his attention and his gaze snapped to mine. "I know it's hard to talk about. We don't have to."

He took a deep breath, chugged down his whiskey, shoved off the couch, and started to pace. "No, it's time I finally talk about it with someone. Rave and I are the only ones that know the real story. It'll be good to get if off my chest."

While pacing he finally dove into the story. "It goes back to when I was fifteen. My parents split when my mom left my father for Rave. He had been here for a few years at that point and had just started running the bar with my uncle, Rich, my mother's brother. My old man was the fucking president and that shit really didn't fly but my mom marched to the beat of her own drum. They didn't get married until I was eighteen, and Rave finally moved in. I guess he wanted the dust to settle with the club a little bit before he stepped on my old man's toes completely."

He poured another three fingers of whiskey in his glass before continuing. "Raine was born shortly after their wedding. Her mom, Colleen, was seventeen, and her folks had kicked her out when I knocked her up. She moved in here and everything was fine. We were one big family. Rave and I even started to get along. It was rough in the club but everything seemed to be smoothing out."

He paused and looked at me, his hands shaking. "I don't think he was a bad person. I think he was driven mad from jealousy and a broken heart." Abel cleared his throat, then took a long swig. "Raine was about a year and a half when it happened. I was working late at the garage and Rave was helping me. He had left his bike in the driveway and rode with me in my truck. I think Rave was the target but just happened to not be home. Anyway, my old man went into our house and shot my mom while she was cleaning up the dishes from dinner. I think Colleen took him by surprise. He shot her too before killing himself. The rest of the night is a fucking blur. The cops came to the garage and my world crumbled. The guilt that has buried itself inside of me and Rave will never go away. In one moment the only two women I'd ever loved were taken by the monster sperm donor who was the president of the club I had grown to love. It was all going to hell in a goddamned handbasket."

I was paralyzed. I had no words. Nothing.

"Abel, I..." He sat down next to me, burying his head in the nape of my neck. I wrapped my arms around him. "I wish I knew what to say."

"Don't say anything. It's all in the past. I'll never get over it, but it is what it is."

CHAPTER 9

O ver the next few weeks we all started to finally get into a groove of normalcy. I started working again, Abel was spending more time at the garage than the bar, and Rave was becoming an afternoon regular for me. I even started picking Raine up from school so she could do her homework while I finished out the day shift so Able could work late.

"Hey, Crickett right?" a surly voice came from the bar top while I was cleaning some glasses.

I looked up to see, Rich, Abel's uncle. I had seen him from time to time, mostly when he was going in and out of the back room or coming in to talk to guys in the back by the pool tables.

"Yes, sir. What can I get you?"

He sat down at the empty seat in front of him. "I'll take Old Crow and Seven Up."

I made his drink and awkwardly stood in front of him, not knowing the first thing to say to strike up a conversation with the president of the club. I always thought of Abel as being my boss, but this was his boss and that made me nervous as shit.

He took a sip. "Ah. That hits the spot. I just wanted to properly welcome you to our little family here. I've been pretty busy since you arrived and I didn't want to seem rude."

I wiped the bar next to him, just to seem like I was staying busy in front of the big boss. "Thanks. I understand. You have a business to run."

Holt walked through the front door and Rich turned to him. They nodded at each other and Holt came behind the bar.

"Well, I better get to the table. Crickett, mind staying a little late today? We might need Holt to go on an errand later."

I shrugged. "Sure, I just have to grab Raine from school. But it shouldn't be a problem."

The front door swung open and Abel strode in with Raine on his back.

"Never mind." I pointed to my two new favorite people in the world. "I don't have to go anywhere."

Raine's eyes got wide when she saw Rich and she raced into his arms for a big bear hug.

Abel leaned on the bar. "Can I see you for a second?" His face was stoic.

"Sure?" I glanced over at Holt. "I'll be right back."

Abel led me over to the small room that we used as a liquor closet and locked the door behind us.

"Is everything ok?"

He didn't waste any time. He threw me against the wall and crushed his lips onto mine.

"I have been thinking about this all day."

I could feel how ready he was pressing hard into my lower stomach. He pulled at the button of my shorts, letting them fall to the floor.

"Abel is this really a good idea?"

He gently bit my neck, running his hand up my shirt to unclasp my bra.

"I think it's one of the best fucking ideas ever."

I fumbled with his zipper. I had to admit that the forbidden-sex-in-the-workplace thing was pretty thrilling.

He went to grab for his wallet and his head fell as he sighed. "I forgot a fucking condom at home."

"That's ok, Abel. I want to feel you."

"Do you really want to feel all of me?"

I knew what he was getting at and I was still nervous, but he said he was clean and in that moment the need to please him outweighed my nerves.

"Yes, I want to feel just you."

"Are you sure you're fine with this?"

"Yes." I stared into his eyes.

He lifted me into his strong arms and I tightened my legs around his waist. Abel pulled my thong to the side and thrust into me, making me gasp.

"Hush. We have to be fast and quiet."

I bit down on the top of his tattooed chest as a groan escaped.

"Abel. Right there."

The tip of his dick was massaging my g-spot perfectly; the fast part was not going to be a problem. My body started to shake in his arms as my climax started to build. His hot breath quickened on my neck as he pressed my back harder into the wall.

"Come for me babe." He growled in my ear and that was all it took.

An uncontrollable wave of ecstasy crashed over me while his cock pulsed inside me. With a sigh his head fell onto my shoulder.

"Fucking amazing," he whispered, setting me back down on my feet. "I will not ever be able to fuck you with a condom on ever again."

I kissed his shoulder as he started to let me out of his arms. "Good."

We straightened out our clothes as Abel kissed me on the cheek and breathed, "Follow my lead."

As he unlocked the door, he yelled, "This isn't over. We will talk about it later."

I jumped right in, storming out of the liquor closet, arms crossed. "Yeah, whatever, Abel. I'm over it."

I got back behind the bar with everyone's eyes darting from me to Abel.

"Trouble in paradise?" Holt chuckled with a swift wink.

"You could call it that, I guess." I started wiping off the bar and the club members started filing into the back room. Abel glanced over at me with a quick grin as he mouthed, "See you later." I nodded and felt blush dust over my neck and cheeks.

Raine scooted down the bar to be right in front of me. "Was Daddy being mean to you?" Her brow was creased and her eyes looked like waterworks were about to start spraying the whole place.

I grabbed her little hand. "Of course not, Raine. He and I were just playing around. Your daddy is a very nice man."

Her lips pulled into a soft smile. "Yeah, he's great. Can I have a soda?"

I poured a Dr. Pepper and started quizzing her on her vocabulary and spelling for her test the next day.

After about thirty minutes with no one coming in,

Holt and I were both helping Raine with homework, trying to pass the time.

"I really don't see why Rich wanted you to stick around."

I shrugged after taking a sip from my water. "It's really no big deal."

He started burning one of the ice troughs. "It's just a waste of your time, that's all."

Abel came busting through the back door. "Holt. We need to see you. Now." His face was gruff, and his tone and posture matched.

I got overly nervous for Holt as he looked over to me with concern dancing across his face. "I guess it is a good thing that you stuck around."

"Crickett, why don't you take Raine home? We won't be too long and this place is dead."

She hopped off the stool and I grabbed the drawer to count it out.

Abel grabbed it from me. "You should really leave now babe. I'll take care of this and bring your tips home tonight."

I was screaming inside to know what was going on, but I just grabbed Raine by the hand and walked her out of the bar.

"Can we have chicken fingers for dinner?"

A light rain tapped onto the gravel parking lot as we

started to jog for my car. "As long as you eat some carrots with them."

I strapped Raine into the backseat and started off toward the house. I hated the jumping, squeaking, skipping wipers, but it was starting to really pour and I needed to try to see the winding road. Even though it was annoying, I would rather the obnoxious noises than being pelted in the face while on a motorcycle.

I was cleaning up the plates from dinner when Holt and Abel finally came home. Both of them were smiling and talking away as their boots stomped through the front door. Then I noticed it: Holt was wearing a cut.

"Well, I guess I had nothing to worry about this whole time." I gave Holt a hug. "Congratulations."

"Thanks." They both grabbed beers from the fridge.

"There's some food in the oven for y'all."

"Thanks babe." Abel pulled me down to sit on his lap at the breakfast table, cracking open a beer for me too. "A toast to our newest member." We smashed our beers together.

"Sorry for kicking you out of the bar like that earlier. I needed to keep this guy on his toes. Didn't want to spoil a good surprise."

I kissed his scruffy cheek. "I get it."

The guys made plates and I curled up on the couch with Raine while they ate. Raine dozed off watching My Little Pony—not the terrible new remake that the crackheads at the network had started airing, the reruns from when I was growing up. I was more enthralled in it than I would have cared to admit; I didn't even notice that she was passed out next to me until I started to fast-forward through a few commercials.

"I guess I better get this little lady in bed." Abel lifted her into his arms before turning to me. "Put some warmer clothes on, let's go for a ride."

"It just stopped raining, the roads will be wet. I don't think it's a good idea."

I hadn't been on Abel's bike since that day we'd gone to the diner. Once was really enough for me. I liked a thrill as much as the next guy, but there was an element of danger that was just a little too much for me.

"Come on. I want to show you something."

I let my head fall onto the couch backrest. "Fine. But if I freak out or scream, it's on you."

CHAPTER 10

The sweet smell of rain-soaked flowers whisked by as we rode down the winding mountain road, twisting and turning farther and farther from town and any section that looked familiar.

Even though it was the middle of May, the night air was chilly even with my jeans and hoodie on. I hugged myself tighter onto Abel as I shrieked a little when he took a sharp corner faster and tighter than I was remotely comfortable with.

He turned off down a dark dirt road in the middle of nowhere, pulling over onto the shoulder. "Babe, there's something I want to show you."

I got off the bike. "Where in God's name are we?"

"Well, we're technically in Tennessee, and this is known to the locals as Compression Falls."

He grabbed my hand as the clouds finally parted, revealing a huge full moon. The damp trees sparkled in the moonlight as Abel led me down a steep path.

"It's not too much farther now."

We finally made our way down to a riverbank and the sound of a roaring waterfall broke into the calm night air. We rolled up our jeans and took our shoes off, wading out to a large, smooth rock closer to the waterfall.

Abel sat, letting me lean back on his chest. We sat for a few minutes in silence, taking in the beautiful power of the cascading waterfall.

"This is gorgeous."

Abel kissed my shoulder. "It really is. This is where I come when I need to get away from it all."

"Thanks for bringing me here. I've never seen something like this."

His arms tightened around me as his chest heaved from a deep breath. "There's something I have been meaning to ask you."

From the top of my head to my toes tensed. I was bracing myself. If he popped the question right then I would probably freak, and not in a good way.

"Do you believe in marriage?"

Not exactly what I was expecting.

"I don't think I do. I feel like if people want to be around each other then a piece of paper shouldn't define it."

His body relaxed a little. "I couldn't agree more."

"Why are you asking me this?"

"Because you're the first person, ever, that I felt was worth binding myself to. Not even Raine's mom had me thinking about wifing her up. I loved her, but it was more because she gave me my daughter. I don't think we would have stayed together otherwise."

I pulled away from him, shifting to sit with my legs crossed so I was looking right at him. "What are you getting at, Abel?"

He rubbed the back of his neck, staring past me to look at the falls. "I'm getting at the fact that I have fallen for you, Crickett. I fucking love you. You're not just some broad or something. You're special."

I leaned in, brushing my lips over his. "I love you too."

"You know…we're all alone, and that water looks mighty nice."

"Wont it be cold as shit?"

He shook his head. "This area is all spring fed. It's pretty much the same temperature all year round."

"Race ya to the waterfall!" I jumped up, stripped down, and sprinted into the water, Abel hot on my tail.

We swam right up under the falling water, Abel holding me up since the bottom was a little too deep for me to stand comfortably.

Slowly we started a high school make out session like

we were two horny kids hiding under the bleachers at a football game.

All of a sudden Abel started busting out laughing.

"What's so funny?"

He quickly kissed me again. "It's just so crazy that two months ago you walked into my life, and now here we are."

"What, making out under a waterfall? Yeah, I wouldn't have pictured this either."

"No, I mean that not too long ago, you weren't in my life, and now I can't picture not having you in it."

Wow. Talk about being sappy. That one hit me right in the feels.

Right then I felt my heart start really beating again. The warmth flooded through me. It was like I finally knew what life was about, what love needed to feel like, what I had been looking for. It was the most breathtaking moment of my life, one that I would never forget.

"I didn't know bikers could be so mushy."

"You just bring it out of me. I'm never this charming in real life."

"This is real life, babe. So you better get used to it, because I like this side of you, especially since it's only for me."

He kissed from my jaw down to my shoulder. "Everything is only for you babe. You and Raine are my world now."

A flood of desire came over me. I reached down and started to stroke him gently. "You know one thing I haven't done?"

He softly breathed into my neck, moaning a little. "What's that?"

"Had sex under a waterfall. That's bucket list status shit right there."

"Well than let's both check one off the list."

He bit lightly on my shoulder and I rubbed his head over my folds, slowly inserting him into my tight opening. He gasped quietly, riding his dick farther and farther into me.

We stayed silent, enjoying the calmness and beauty of the moment. For the first time since we'd started whatever it was we were, we weren't just fucking each other for the pleasure of it. We were making love. It was a night neither of us would ever forget.

The ride back to the house was a little more miserable than the ride there since I was freezing. The temperature continued to drop, and combining that with my wet hair and damp clothes, I was not the happiest of campers. Even so, it was a small price to pay for the amazing time we'd had at Compression Falls.

———

I WAS YAWNING up a storm the next morning on my way

to the bar. Abel had left before I was even out of bed, saying that he had some club business he needed to handle. Raine was fed and off to school, and now it was time to start another eight hour shift.

Of all the days for Abel to not call someone into work for me. I pulled into the parking lot to see two vans I didn't recognize surrounded by a bunch of the club members' bikes. I knew better than to let my suspicions start to fly, but it was odd that there were so many people there at that time of day.

I grabbed my sneakers from the trunk while watching two of the younger members rush in through the side door, one of the off limits zones for me.

I unlocked the front door and started setting up like it was just another day at work. I cut limes, filled the ice bins, unwrapped the liquor bottle tops, and counted out my drawer.

The first few hours of the shift were completely dead; not a soul came into the bar or out of the back room. Thank goodness for Tetris and Candy Crush on my phone.

Suddenly the back door swung open and Abel stomped out. His face was twisted into one of the ugliest, most stressed out looks I had ever seen.

"You all right?" I questioned as he stood at the end of the bar staring off out the front window.

"Just give me some whiskey babe. It's one of those days."

I took the hint, poured him some Jack on the rocks, and watched him chug the double shot like it was water.

"Do you have your gun?"

My heart started racing. Why the hell would he be asking me something like that?

I nodded. "It's in the car."

He held out his hand. "Keys."

I threw them to him from my purse under the register. "Should I be worried?"

"No. I just want you to keep it with you while you're working. That's all."

He went and grabbed my gun from the glove box, put it on the bar, and without another word he was back with the rest of them doing God-knows-what. Needless to say I was freaking out. I put my gun in my hip holster. It had been so long since I had even shot my gun, having it on me felt so wrong.

Another hour or so passed by with me trying to occupy my time with silly YouTube videos and scrolling through ideas for another tattoo.

When the front door swung open, I almost jumped out of my skin. A biker wearing a cut that I didn't recognize bellied up to the bar. He had a sweet smile and kind, light brown eyes. He sat down in front of me and sighed as he set his gun on the bar.

I was frozen. I put my hand on my hip, ready to rip my gun from its holster, but he shook his head. "That would be a stupid move, sweetheart." His sweet smile turned into a stoic frown as he eyed me up and down. "You're a pretty little thing aren't you? What's your name?"

I faked a smile. "I'm Crickett. Haven't seen you in here before. What's your name?"

He grabbed the gun and started eyeing it, playfully pointing it just past me. He was trying to freak me out and it was working, but I knew I couldn't let him see that.

"Are you going to order something?"

I stood there with my hands on my hips, begging my knees to stop shaking as I sweetly smiled and glared into his hollow eyes. "Why don't you grab me a Miller Lite."

I poured his draft and set his beer down on a coaster. "That'll be three bucks."

He handed me a five. "Keep the change." He proceeded to chug the entire sixteen ounces.

I was begging for Abel to come back, for any of the guys to walk through the back door, but they never came.

The stranger picked the gun up and pointed it straight at me. "Play time is over. You're going to do everything I tell you or I will blow your brains out."

I nodded. I knew that there was no way I could pull my gun out, turn off the safety, pull the slide back, and shoot him before he shot me, so I had to play by his rules. I was just so thankful that Raine was safely in school.

"First, put your gun on the counter."

I did as I was told and surprisingly he left it where I set it down.

"Now you're going to show me where they're keeping Reggie."

At first I thought he was talking about weed, but it quickly sunk in that he thought I knew where one of his friends was being kept captive.

What that fuck is going on?

My throat was dry and my hands were shaking. "I have no idea who you're talking about."

He jumped off the stool and came around to the inside of the bar. "Don't play fucking dumb with me you little cunt. Now show me where they are."

I had to take him somewhere and I was hoping that he was completely wrong and no one was being held hostage in the back room of the bar. In my mind, I was about to lead him right to a big round table where Abel would pull a gun out and rescue me from this terrible person and his fucked up misunderstanding.

Slowly I shuffled my quivering legs to the back door, gripping the handle. I felt him press the barrel of the gun into the middle of my back.

"What are you waiting for? Open the damn door." His voice was low and level.

I turned the handle to reveal a scene that was so far from the picture I'd had in my mind. There was a large round table shoved off to the left to make room for the group of guys circling a gagged and tied up man who was badly beaten. His face was bloody and swollen.

Abel was standing behind him with a gun to his head, yelling at the guy. "Don't think I won't pull the damn trigger. Now tell me where it is."

I choked out, "Abel!" as the stranger's grip tightened around my body and the barrel pressed to my temple.

His face went white as his eyes locked onto mine. The hostage's head hung while he moaned in pain, spitting blood onto the floor.

"Let her go or your buddy here gets it." Abel seethed.

The Unacceptables that were there were standing frozen, their eyes darting from mine to Abel's.

"Don't think I won't kill her." He breathed in close to my neck. "It's a shame to waist such a fine rack though." I heard the hammer pull back and the bullet move into the chamber. I braced myself, taking in a slow deep breath.

Abel's nostrils flared and he slammed the back of the gun into his hostage's temple. "Don't be a fucking idiot. Let the girl go, she has nothing to do with this."

All of a sudden the sound of a gun firing, someone gasping for air, and the feeling of hot wetness being splattered all over me happened within seconds. It took me a minute to realize what had happened as the grip on my body loosened and the gun was no longer pressed against my head.

I could feel myself screaming as I looked down to see blood covering my body and my attacker lying at my feet motionless. Holt was holding one of the bar knives in his bloody hand. He grabbed me and pulled me into the main area of the bar as my eyes locked onto the man strapped to the chair, half of his head missing and splattered all over the floor in front of him and Abel running toward me.

My attacker was sprawled on the floor in the doorway, blood gushing from his sliced neck as gurgling noises rang out into the air.

I started to fight and struggle in Holt's arms. "Let go of me."

"No. Crickett you have to calm down." He was pulling me behind the bar. "Let me clean you up a bit."

Abel was right behind us, trying to reach out to me. "Both of you get the fuck away from me. You're a fucking monster Abel!"

I stomped on Holt's foot, making his grip on me loosen. I grabbed my gun and my bag and started to run for the door. Abel bolted after me, grabbing my arm right as I was about to shove the heavy wooden door open.

"Crickett. Wait. Don't leave like this."

"Fuck you, Abel. You just killed a man and I almost died." I pulled the hammer back on my gun, keeping it pointed at the ground. "So help me God, Abel. Let go of my fucking arm. I need a little bit of time to process things."

His face twisted and his jaw clenched. "Fine." He let me go and I bolted to my car.

CHAPTER 11

I sped off down the road, my mind going a mile a
minute. My plan was to go back to his place, clean
myself up, grab my shit, and stay at the motel for
the night.

I pulled down the gravel road as my phone started
blowing up with text after text from Abel.

Abel: Babe. Go home. I will be there soon.

Abel: Please call me. We need to talk.

Abel: I am so sorry.

Abel: Crickett, I love you. Please call me.

I threw my phone onto the passenger seat and pulled
a U-turn. If Abel was on his way to the house, there was
no way I was going to be there when he showed up.

I tried to not think about the blood that was drying
on my arms, clothes, legs, and neck, but when I looked

down to see my chest covered in that man's blood, it running down my V-neck all the way to the top of my shorts, I started to go into a panic. I tried taking long, slow breaths, but to no avail.

My body was shaking, my breathing was out of control, and my mind was a jumbled mess.

My phone started blaring and I pulled off to the side of the road to see who it was.

I was surprised at how disappointed I was to not see Abel's or Rave's number coming up. I let the unknown number go to voicemail and leave a message.

I slid my phone open and the message started playing. "Hi, Crickett. This is Cindy, your mom's neighbor. She asked me not to call anyone but I think you really need to get to the hospital quickly. She was mugged. I'm not too sure what really happened, but I found her this morning in really rough shape. The doctors won't give me any information since I am not family and I have to go to work now, but call me if you get an update. She's at Jackson on Fifth. I don't know if they put her in a room or not."

I went into autopilot. In just over twelve hours I could be at my mother's bedside. My tank was full, my adrenaline was pumping, and the radio was blasting. I drove for just over three hours before I stopped at a quiet rest stop. Grabbing the hoodie from the back seat and throwing it over my bloodstained body, I rushed into the bathroom without anyone noticing the dark red that was splattered down my leg.

I locked myself in the handicapped stall and scrubbed my skin raw, threw out my white V-neck and soaked bra, and threw back on my hoodie. My black shorts didn't show the stains too badly, thankfully. It took everything in my power not to picture the wide eyes of the dead man lying at my feet. Even though he'd had no problems with threatening my life, it didn't change the fact that I felt bad that his had been ended. He was someone's son, probably someone's lover or even a father.

After filling up and grabbing a Red Bull, I was back on my mission. After ignoring over twenty calls from Rave and Abel, stopping a few more times for gas, and chugging a handful of energy drinks, I was finally pulling into the parking lot at the hospital.

The security guard was sitting behind the desk. She made a copy of my license, gave me my visitor's pass, and explained the maze I was going to have to go through to get to my mother's room.

Everything felt like it was moving in slow motion. I couldn't believe I was back in my hometown, about to see my mother battered and bruised from another mugging. The guilt of running out on her was overwhelming as I gasped for breath and pushed open the hospital room door.

Right as I was about to take my first step into the

room a nurse stopped me. "Ma'am, only family can go in there, and it's not visiting hours for this floor."

I cleared my throat, turning to the older lady who was standing there with a vial of medication and syringe in hand. "She's my mother," I muttered.

With a kind smile, she nodded. "Have you spoken to the doctor yet?"

I shook my head. "I was out of town. I got the news from a neighbor and drove more than twelve hours straight through to get here."

"Let me give your mother her pain meds and then I will page the doctor for you. I am sure he is going to want to talk with you about her condition."

I followed the nurse in to see my mother lying helpless in the bed. Her face was so swollen and bruised that I barely recognized her. She was hooked up to monitors and IVs, and her right leg was in a cast from the knee down.

I gasped for air as I rushed to her bedside. "What the hell happened?" I pleaded, but my words fell on deaf ears. The nurse had already left and my mom was passed out.

It only took a few minutes for the doctor to come into the room, but it had felt like years.

"Miss Hayes, may we speak in the hall?"

I followed the doctor out of the room. "Doctor, do you know what happened to her?"

He looked over her chart with a furrowed brow. "Your

mother's neighbor found her like this. Your mother said she was raped and mugged but could not give the name of her attacker. She has a few broken ribs and they almost broke her jaw. Her right leg looked to have been stomped on with a steel toe boot; her tibia and fibula are shattered. She's lucky to be alive."

I felt weak. My knees were about to give out. I leaned back on the wall. "I just can't believe this. Is she going to be all right?"

He nodded, trying to smile. "She's doing better. She's stable now. We have her on some pretty heavy pain meds right now to help her rest. She should hopefully be able to go home tomorrow if nothing changes."

"Thank you doctor."

Exhaustion started to take its toll while I sat in the arm chair in the corner of the room, watching my mother take shallow, labored breaths. The next thing I knew, it was the middle of the night and a blaring alarm was going off. I shot up out of the chair and ran over to my mother's side as the night nurse came rushing through the door.

The nurse pushed some buttons, fixed a few things. My mom groaned as the nurse put the oxygen tube back in her nose. "Your oxygen levels started dropping. You need to keep this on."

Through slits, my mom glanced at me. "What are you

doing here?" she muttered, but before I could answer she was falling back into her drug fueled daze.

The nurse patted my shoulder. "She'll be more with it tomorrow. Try to get a little more rest."

Hot coals felt like they were embedded in my lower back as I tried to make the best out of the uncomfortable chair. After I flipped through the limited channels for a while, thumbed through a few magazines, and did a crossword puzzle, my eyelids finally started to get heavy.

The sound of coughing brought me out of a light sleep. I shot up from the chair to find my mother staring wide-eyed at me.

"Well, look what the cat dragged in." She rolled her eyes, trying to sit up more in her bed.

I ambled over to her bedside, trying to rub out a kink in my shoulder and neck. "I came as soon as I heard you were hurt, Ma."

"Don't even feel the need to tell your momma that you're leaving but you feel like you have to come here and play hero? My dear, you're not needed here." Her bloodshot eyes were boring into my soul.

"I'm sorry I ran out on you like that. I just couldn't get stuck in the quicksand of that life forever."

She hit the call button for the nurse before glaring at me. "Don't get self-righteous on me, Crit. We don't have to do this. You made your choice. Run back off to wherever you came from. I can take care of myself." Her words were mumbled from her jaw being so sore.

"Obviously." I twirled my finger around the room. "You can totally take care of yourself, Ma."

The nurse came in. "Morning, Helen. How are you feeling today?"

"Like I got hit by a truck."

CHAPTER 12

After the nurse left the room, my mother started to give me the good ole fashioned silent treatment. All the way through the doctor coming in, explaining the aftercare instructions, and discharging her—which took hours—my mom didn't speak one word to me.

It wasn't until we were in the car on the way back to the trailer that she graced me with conversation. "So where'd you run off to? Find a man?"

I rolled my eyes. "I went to find dad."

She forced a laugh. "That deadbeat. I bet he's dead in some ditch somewhere."

"I found him."

I could see her pissed off face out of the corner of my eye. "And?"

"He's doing well. It was surprising to find him with hundreds of letters and page after page of legal papers. Why the fuck did you let me think that he had abandoned me for all those years? Don't you know what that did to me?"

"He walked out on us, Crit. Don't let that slime ball ever try to fool you into thinking otherwise."

"Let's just leave it. We're not going to agree."

I helped her hobble into the trailer and propped her leg up on the couch with a couple of pillows like the nurse had explained to me before we left.

"Get me my damn pills."

I grabbed her purse out of her reach. "You can't take one for at least another hour, Ma. You know that. And you have to eat with them."

"Fuck you. You're not the boss of me."

I was over it. All of the feelings of guilt for leaving her washed away as she looked at me with complete loathsome disgust. I looked around the tiny living room of our trailer, which was falling apart. The two buckets were nearly full of water from the roof leaks, the mildew was stinking up the place from carpet that had needed to be replaced years before, and the furniture was falling apart and mismatched, but none of that bothered me. The fact that the stove hadn't worked right since I was fifteen was fine, and the way that the faucet in the bathroom made a glugging sound while it ran wasn't the issue. The biggest problem in that whole dilapidated place was the woman who'd settled for that shithole so many years before. She was the problem with my life that I was running away from. She was the wretched quicksand that tried to suck my life away. My mother was a miserable excuse for a human being. I had known it for years, but I was finally letting myself be at peace with it.

I handed her the bag and started to dial the pizza place just up the road. "If you're going to insist on abusing your medications, then at least eat something so you don't destroy what little liver you have left."

I barely got her to eat half a slice of pizza before she was popping two more pills into her mouth and falling asleep on the couch with a lit cigarette between her lips.

I pulled a blanket over her, put out the cigarette, and decided to call it a night. She had taken enough medication to keep her knocked out for the night and the walls were thin enough that if she needed me, I would be able to hear her.

The feeling of my old room, my old sheets and bed, my old everything was awful. I hated how stifling being back there was. My phone vibrated with another unread text from Abel. I powered it down; there was only so much drama I could handle for one day.

I knew that he was worried about me and that it was probably wrong to ignore him the way that I was, but the image of him killing a man in cold blood right in front of me was something that was not going to go away easily. I wasn't completely naive; I knew that it was the nature of the beast. Abel was the freaking vice president of the motorcycle club for crying out loud. I had seen a few episodes of Sons of Anarchy, I knew there was probably blood on his hands, but knowing it was probable and knowing it was fact were two very different animals in my book. Ignorance really was bliss.

I woke up to a loud crash coming from the living room around five in the morning. I grabbed the robe that hung on the back of my door and raced to my mother's side. She was laying on the couch, her eyes barely open, drool dripping from the left side of her mouth. She had knocked the side table over trying to shove up from the couch without her crutches.

"Do you need to go to the bathroom?" I asked, putting my arm under hers, ready to hoist her up. That's when I saw the almost empty bottle of pills lying open on the floor next to my feet.

Horror rushed in. "Mom, oh my God! You didn't." She slurred a few words that I was unable to make out as I shook her. I looked down to her hand: she was gripping a syringe full of what I figured to be heroine.

"Mom what the fuck do you think you're doing? This is not the answer." I kept shaking her and she came to a little bit more.

"Please, Crit. I'm so tired." Her head rolled onto my shoulder and I sat down next to her, silently panicking.

She groggily patted my thigh. "I don't want to fight anymore." Her words slurred together as her eyes struggled to stay open.

My voice cracked as I tried to figure out what to do. "Mom, you can turn this around. Let me help you get out of this hellhole."

"Honey, it's too late." Her drool was dripping onto my arm as she started to position the needle to her vein. "There's nothing in this world left for me. They've taken it all from me. I have nothing left."

I was like a deer in headlights, just waiting in the middle of the road for the accident to happen through the tears welling in my eyes. Slowly she pushed the drugs into her bloodstream. I knew that she was done. I knew that I should have been calling the police, but I just sat there paralyzed while I watched my mother take her own shitty life. The worst part, the part that really scared me, was that I wasn't surprised. I wasn't sad. I was just numb. Maybe deep down I knew that it was all for the best, and if that was what she really wanted then who was I to stand in her way?

I cradled her in my arms while she shook, tears rolling down her swollen, bruised face.

"I love you." It was the first time in years that I had said those words to her.

"Love you too, Crickett." Her eyes rolled back in her head as her slurred words faded. Her last breath was shallow, fleeting. I felt her leave, and I crumbled.

For what felt like hours, I held her in my arms and cried. Really it was only about twenty minutes before banging started on the front door as Abel's and Rave's yelling called to me.

I just sat there, scared to let them into the horrifying scene that I was entrenched in. Part of me didn't want to open the door because once that happened, it all would be real. The whole nightmare of the past few days would all be too real for me to deal with.

It didn't take long for Abel to kick in the front door. I was still a blubbering statue, clinging to my mother's lifeless body as they busted into the trailer. The light flooded in from the open door, stinging my eyes as they rushed to my side.

Rave grabbed my mom and Abel scooped me into his arms. "Oh, fuck, babe what happened?" I fell apart in his arms. No words would form. It was all just too much.

Rave repositioned my mom onto the couch. He rubbed the back of his neck while he stared down at her. "I have to call the cops, Crickett. We have to get this taken care of."

Abel whispered, "You didn't…?"

I gasped and smacked his chest, pushing away from him with the little energy that I had left. "Who the fuck do you think I am? Do you really think I would kill my own mother?"

"Babe, don't take it the wrong way. I had to ask. We don't know what happened here."

Rave put his hand on my shoulder. "I think we need to have a little chat, sweetheart. I know it's hard, but you need to let us help you right now."

I followed them into the kitchen, the three of us taking seats around the table. Through light sobbing I told them the whole roller coaster I had been on since I'd stormed out of the bar the day before.

"All right. Here's what's going to happen." Rave started to pace around the kitchen. "I am going to call the cops and we're going to tell them the truth, that Helen offed herself, that Crickett came to take care of her, and that we were just showing up to help out too. No lying, no crazy stories to keep straight. They might ask a lot of questions, but no one can get in trouble here, so there's nothing to worry about."

Rave walked outside to make the call, leaving Abel and I awkwardly sitting in the kitchen staring blankly at the walls.

"I am so sorry about yesterday, babe."

I grabbed his hand. "I know you'd never put me in danger, Abel, but the life you live is dangerous. And the fact that you killed that man, it just haunts me."

He weaved his fingers with mine. "I will do anything to make it up to you."

I took in a deep slow breath and crawled into his lap. "Just love me."

I was too tired, too shook up, and too in love with him to fight or push him away any more. He had driven almost thirteen hours to fight for me. It was the first time I experienced what that truly felt like, someone loving me enough to stop at nothing to get me back.

He sighed into me, kissing the top of my head. "You're mine. I'm never letting you go again."

EPILOGUE

ONE YEAR LATER

My body shook from pleasure as Abel's thrusts sent my body into a hyper drive of euphoria. Our climaxes crashed around us and I fell onto the bed, a light layer of sweat coating my tired body.

Abel settled down behind me, slowly planting small kisses on my shoulder blade. "How was that, Mrs. Hellock?"

I rolled over in his arms, drowning in the ocean blue eyes of my new husband. "Are you ever going to stop calling me that?"

He shrugged. "Maybe when the shock of it wears off. So probably never."

I laughed a little. "How about Rave's or Raine's shock

when we tell them that our little trip to Florida was actually a shotgun trip to Vegas?"

Abel looked at me, blankly trying to piece together what I meant.

I kissed his cheek. "Why do you think I agreed to come here this weekend and cancel our plans in the Keys?"

"Are you serious?"

I planted a gentle kiss on his lips. "I found out a week ago. You really couldn't figure it out?"

He shook his head. "I had no idea."

"I've been sleepy and a little queasy in the mornings. I didn't even touch the champagne that Elvis impersonator handed me last night."

"Holy shit, we're having a baby. We just got married and we're having a fucking kid." The smile that spread over his face was like a contagious wildfire of excitement. "Mrs. Hellock, I think you have just made me the fucking happiest man in the entire world. Hands down."

I hugged him to me. "You're okay with having another child?"

He looked deep into my eyes. "I cannot wait. I love you so much, babe."

"I love you too, Abel. With my whole heart."

We called for room service and looked out over the flashing bright lights of the Vegas Strip.

Abel grabbed my hand and pulled me into him while I stood by the window watching all the tourists rushing from the bars and casinos. It looked like a swarm of bees trying to find honey.

"Are you happy?" he whispered in my ear.

I pulled his arms tighter around my body. "I don't think I could be any happier."

I stared down at the rings resting on our fingers. It was all so overwhelming. Something that I'd sworn I would never do completely fulfilled me in that moment. I had never wanted anything more than to be his, only his, and with one hasty trip to Sin City we had made the ultimate commitment. It should have scared the shit out of me, but I had never been so calm and sure about anything in my entire life. Abel Hellock was meant to be mine and I was meant to be his.

He kissed my shoulder before asking, "What are you thinking about, babe?"

I laughed a little to myself. "Honestly, I was just thinking about that night you told me you'd be my Prince Charming if I needed one."

He chuckled a little. "Yeah, I remember that."

I sighed into him. "I didn't realize it then, but I really did need one, and I am thankful it was you who saved me."

"I think you're the one that saved me, sugar."

I turned to kiss his soft lips. "Forget the horse, my Prince Charming rides a motorcycle."

The End.

DID YOU ENJOY WHAT YOU JUST READ?

RATE IT: If the answer is yes, you did enjoy Unacceptable, please consider putting up a review. Writing a review for an author is like tipping a server at a restaurant, even the bad ones are better than nothing.

SHARE IT: Please help spread the word about Unacceptable. Tell your friends and family about it or share it with them. Sharing is caring, after all.

STAY CONNECTED: Follow Kristen Hope Mazzola on **http://www.facebook.com/khmazz.author** or **twitter.com/khmazz** to stay up to date about new releases, giveaways, and so much more! Join Kristen's email mailing list for her monthly newsletter: kristenhopemazzola.-

com/mailing-list.html and there is always Kristen's Street Team to join on Facebook: **Kristen Hope Mazzola's Rockstars**!

ACKNOWLEDGMENTS

To my amazing readers: You all are what keep me going. Your unbelievable support and encouragement are instrumental in my creative process and I do not know what I would do without each and every one of you!

Author BFFs: Y'all know who you are and you are all my heroes! Thank you for keeping my head on straight and reminding me why I am an author. Without each and every one of you ladies, I don't know if I would still be doing what I love and for that I am eternally thankful!

C. Marie: I really hope you know how much I have grown to admire and respect how much better you make my writing. You're guidance helps make my books the best they can be and I don't think you will ever know how much that means to me. You take the coal I give you and polish into the diamond that it deserves to be.

Brittainy C. Cherry: You're a rock star and an ever present light of inspiration for me. I don't know what I would do without your help, support and friendship! You really are one of the best friends I have ever had and I am so thankful that this crazy book world has brought us together! You're talented beyond words and the sweetest person ever!

WANT MORE OF THE UNACCEPTABLES?

The Unacceptables MC Series is made up of steamy, gritty, standalone romances focusing on the Unacceptables Motorcycle club! From the presidents of the chapters, to their swoon-worthy club members, to the old ladies that are the backbone of the club - this series has it all, with tons of characters that will rev your engine while melting your heart, keeping you turning those pages... So, grab your e-reader and get your heart racing while falling in love with this amazing group of hardcore bikers and their entire family as they take you on one hell of a wild ride!

UNACCEPTABLE

It's finally my time.

Time to escape from my mother, her crazy antics and questionable morals. I'm getting the heck out of Dodge, leaving the trailer park, to make something of myself. Everything was fine until I walked into The Unacceptables' bar and met Abel Hellock. With his gorgeous muscles, tattoos, motorcycle and perfect smile, my knees quaked. My life was about to be sucked back into the seedy underbelly I fought so desperately to climb out of.

Everything was fine until I met my step-brother for the first time.

————

UNSPEAKABLE

It's finally my time...

Everyone has their damn breaking point, why did the president of my MC's daughter have to be mine? She was everything I wanted, and nothing I could have. Being a prospect was hard enough. Living with my father that I had only known for a few years wasn't making life any easier. And there I was, ready to jeopardize it all for love. I went to Vilas to figure out where I came from, little did I know that I wasn't just going to be passing through. This life was pumping through my veins my whole life, I just didn't know it until I walked into the Unacceptable's bar for the first time.

Raine Hellock was my kryptonite and come hell or high water, I was going to figure out how to make her mine.

———

Unbreakable

The life I live is a dangerous one:
I am the wife of an outlaw.
The daughter of the Unacceptables' President.
But it's finally our time. Time to truly start our life. With our first baby on the way, Ryder and my life could not be more perfect.
The club is doing well and the family is stronger than ever. But, is it all too good to be true?
After all, I am their kryptonite and they will stop at nothing to protect me and my child. Can Ryder and the rest of his club be enough to keep us safe?

———

Untouchable

The life I live is a dangerous one:
I am an outlaw.

A proud member of the Unacceptables MC.
Our club is a family and we will do anything to protect it
- and I mean anything.
The dust was finally settling from our last war. I was
sober, the MC was healing from our loss, and life was
getting back to normal. But regicide cannot go
unpunished.
And when a newcomer arrives and threatens all that we
hold dear...well, he better watch his back, because...
I am Trent Laurence.
I will stop at nothing to protect what I believe in.

————

UNBEARABLE

It is finally my time.
I am an outlaw. The president of the Atlanta charter of
the Unacceptables MC.
You can call me Bear.
I've given my blood, sweat, and life to my club. Devotion
is a complete understatement.
It wasn't until a cute blonde walked into my garage that I
considered giving myself to anything else.
Her perfect smile drew me in. Her sass made me crazy.
I'll do anything to protect my MC - and now her.

———

Undeniable

Ryan Axston may have been my brother's best friend, but
he is so much more than that to me...
He was my first everything. Kiss. Sexual encounter. Love.
Ax had my whole heart, but he had no freaking clue.

He always wanted to be a Marine. It was in his blood.
The day his brother was shipped home in a body bag, Ax
signed up and left town to do his duty to his country.
I forced myself to move on. I really thought he was gone
forever.

When he showed back up wearing the Unacceptables'
skull and bones on his back ten years later, I thought I'd
be able to fight all the old feelings I had for Ax. I was
older, wiser, and unofficial godmother to my best friend's
adorable little girl, Annie.

But all he had to do was crook his finger and it was as if I
was 17 all over again. I wasn't willing to sit back and let
him tear us apart again. This time I was going to fight for
what I wanted. But not even my love could stop a bullet.
One of us was going to have to make a life-altering
choice. Would it be me, or him?

———

UNTAMED

Available exclusively in The Unacceptables Series Box Set

I am the Butcher.
I am an enforcer for the Unacceptables MC.
There are choices we make that we can never come back
from and I have to live with the consequences of mine.
I am Rave.
I am the loving father of a little five year old girl.
There came a day when I had to walk away from everything
I loved and I am going to stop at nothing to make this right.

———

UNCUT

He was a former Marine.
He used to be an enforcer for the Unacceptables MC.
Ryan Axston gave up everything for love - for me. His
patch, his gun, everything he thought he wanted in life.
He claims that nothing compares to our perfect new life.
But is everything too perfect?
Could an outlaw really walk away completely?

––––––

Unscarred

It is finally our time.

He's an outlaw. The president of the Atlanta charter of the Unacceptables MC.

I'm his old lady – devoted, strong, and ready for anything.

But was I ready for what was coming?

Everything was perfect, or so it seemed.

It wasn't until a bone chilling knock at our door that I considered running.

Our perfect life was about to be shattered.

He'd do anything to protect me and his club. But was it enough to really keep everyone safe?

––––––

Unstable

It's finally my time... I am an outlaw.

The proud right-hand man to the president in the Unacceptables MC.

I wasn't prepared for the curveball life was about to throw at me. But if there is one thing I have learned from being in my organization: you have to be ready for anything.

When Ryder showed up on my doorstep, I wasn't sure if I could handle it. I didn't know how to be a father.

I am Holt Walsh, and this is my story.

————

TIS THE SEASON

It's finally my time.

I am an outlaw. The son of Abel Hellock. The legacy of my club.

They all called me too sweet for the life. My club was losing faith in me and the entire organization. I had to prove to them and myself that I was the man my father would have wanted me to be.

When the holidays rolled around, I was more Scrooge than Jolly Saint Nick. That is until she tested me: a girl that I didn't know but I needed to protect. I wasn't prepared for how my life was about to change. But if there is one thing I have learned from being in my organization: you have to be ready for anything.

I am Collin Hellock and this is my story.

————

UNFIXABLE

It is finally my time.

I am the vice president of the Arkansas charter of the
Unacceptables MC.
I'm Reese. I'm an outlaw. A heretic dirt-bag who only
cares about one thing – my club. I'm what they
call....unfixable.

Well, that all was true until she came to town.
She's a white light in a sea of darkness.

I had no idea that her past could become my undoing –
but I didn't care. I would stop at nothing to protect her.
To right all of those wrongs. To remove the despair from
her sweet eyes.

I am a protector of my MC...and now her.

UNKILLABLE
*Available exclusively in the bestselling Love, Loyalty
& Mayhem Charity Anthology*

It's finally my time... I am an outlaw.

They say that I am unkillable. That is my sole claim to fame in my world and one that I proudly honor.

I am the president of the Arkansas Chapter of the merciless Unacceptables MC.

I am a single father.

I am a leader.

I am a killer.

I will stop at nothing to protect my family, but will my reputation precede me or will fate ultimately catch up with me?

I am Maccon Allred, and this is my story.

*Note: All romances in the Unacceptables MC series are intended for ages 18+ due to sexual situations, language, and adult content.

ABOUT THE AUTHOR

Wall Street Journal and *USA Today* bestselling author, Kristen Hope Mazzola, is a Florida native that has found herself loving a North Carolina life. She writes contemporary romance ranging from steamy romantic comedy, sexy erotica, angsty new adult, all the way to sports romance – with dirty bikers, hot military men, and swoon-worthy rockstars in between.

Stay Connected
www.KristenHopeMazzola.com
AuthorKristenMazzola@gmail.com

ALSO BY KRISTEN HOPE MAZZOLA

The Crashing Series:

Crashing: The Wedding

Crashing Back Down

Falling Back Together

Crash & Burn

The Hysterics Standalone Series:

The Hysterics

Colt & Serena

Becoming Hysteric

Steele

The Unacceptables MC Standalone Series:

Unacceptable

Unspeakable

Unbreakable

Untouchable

Unbearable

Undeniable

Untamed (*Available exclusively in The Unacceptables Series Box*

Set One)

Uncut

Unscarred

Unstable

Tis The Season

Unfixable

Unkillable (*Available exclusively in the bestselling Love, Loyalty & Mayhem Anthology*)

Shots On Goal Standalone Series:

Hat Trick

Cross Checked

Cherry Picked

Low Blow

Playoff Beard

Off Duty

For You, I Will

First Last Kiss

The Happy Hour Standalone Series:

Manhattan

Gin & Tonic

Dirty Martini

Cosmopolitan

Standalones:

Stupid Hearts

Rough & Tumble

Donut Be Easy

Offsides

Boxsets:

The Crashing Series

Lust & Love

The Shots on Goal Series Box Set

The Unacceptables Series Box Set One

The Unacceptables Series Box Set Two

The Hysterics: A Rock Star Standalone Box Set

First Timers: The Box Set

The Huntress Series (co-written with Dawn Robertson):

The Huntress (Book 1)

The Hopeless (Book 2)

The Nameless (Book 3)

Charity Compilations:

30 Dirty Martinis

Word Search For Warriors: Authors For A Cause (Volume 1)

Love, Loyalty & Mayhem Anthology

The 69 Series:

(multi-author collaborations for charity)

Hook & Ladder 69

Bleed Blue 69

www.ingramcontent.com/pod-product-compliance
Lightning Source LLC
Chambersburg PA
CBHW021155130626
46554CB00005B/1827